Once Upun a Time
A Book of Puns and Other Nonsense

By Holly Geely

DEDICATION

For Papa, because I blame you for my sense of humour.

CONTENTS

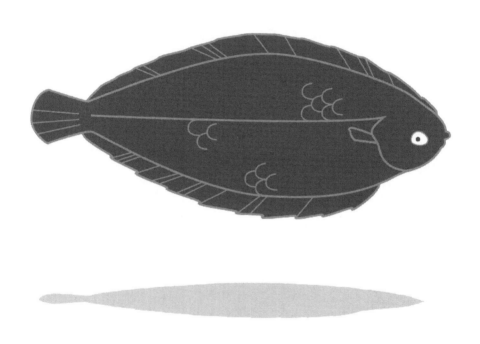

PART 1: ONCE UPUN A TIME
Frivolous Fantasy Fiction

HAPPY BIRTHDAY, ZEUS!

Zeus raised his mug of alcoholic Ambrosia. It twinkled in the moonlight like a plethora of shiny diamonds, plucked from the mines of Gaea below. Zeus' wife had arranged this feast ages in advance and had pulled out all the stops. He was sure the other gods would be impressed and Hera would feel good about herself. Zeus, on the other hand, was ready for a toast.

"Here's to victory!" he bellowed.

The gods clinked mugs and knocked back their first drink. Once it had settled into their divine bellies, the party finally started. Aphrodite had shed the tiny shell bra that made up most of her outfit, and she was dancing on the table with her husband. Hephaestus had taken up her discarded seashells and was using them as a hat. It was rather fetching.

Zeus' wife leaned his way. She had a perfectly pleasant smile on her face so becoming it was almost convincing. Their extended family was well aware of the venom in her veins and wouldn't have been fooled. The truth was, nobody cared.

"What victory were you toasting specifically?" Hera asked.

Zeus tried to maintain his cool façade. Sometime the sunglasses helped, but he felt sweat trickling down his nose.

"Nothing particular, dear."

Hera's eyes narrowed slightly, though the sparkling smile remained.

"You got laid again last night, didn't you?" she said.

Zeus spat out his mouthful of ambrosia. Apollo squawked in protest when the liquid stained his toga.

"What? No, of course not," Zeus said. Hera could tell he was lying because his Ambrosia was foaming around his mouth.

"Chug, chug, chug!" howled Dionysus. Athena wiggled her eyebrows and polished off an entire barrel.

"I remember the days we sipped wine instead of chugged, and we sat around like proper gods," Hestia said. As the eldest, it was her duty to be the most civilized, and bring some class to the party. She couldn't believe Athena's nerve; she was the goddess of wisdom, not drunken carryings-on. She expected Demeter to agree with her and waited to be praised for her insight.

"Don't be such a sour old grape, old woman," Demeter said.

"*Old grape?* I'll show you old grape, you mother of a pomegranate-chugging glutton!" Hestia pulled a couple of slaughtered sheep out of her sacrifice handbag and pelted them at her younger sister. Demeter howled and beat her chest a few times before retaliating with water guns (filled with her special mixture of grains and various earth-poisons).

"Fight! Fight! FIIIIGHT!" Ares screamed.

Zeus signaled to Poseidon. The rowdiness of the crowd drowned out his voice, but Poseidon could read lips. He cracked open the emergency case and hit the red button. Alarm sirens wailed throughout the mountain.

"By the *us*, what are you doing?" Zeus demanded.

"You said release the kraken," Poseidon said.

"Why on Grandmother would I want you to release the kraken during a party? You buffoon! I said release the *crackers*!"

"Crackers?"

"I wish for something salty to go with this splendid cheese!"

"Shit," Poseidon said.

"Do you hear terrified screaming?" Hades asked. Ah, terror. How he loved it. And oh, how he missed it. Since he got married, he'd gone soft, or at least that's what all his ghoulish minions insisted. He looked at Persephone beside him and felt all gooey inside.

"You've got shit on your face," she said, though she hadn't bothered to look up from her cell phone.

"I love you," Hades sobbed.

The golden tiles of the dining room rumbled beneath them.

"Shit," Poseidon said again.

"What have you done this time?" Zeus asked.

"Well, and I *am* sorry about this, but I've just remembered where I left Susan."

"Susan?"

"Yes, Susan. Krakens have names too, you know."

"Sure, but Susan?"

"That's not the issue here, Ares," Zeus said. "Where did you leave her, you oversized trout?"

"She was taking a swim under the - "

Massive tentacles erupted through the table. One long sucker-covered appendage wrapped around Hermes' waist. The tentacle squeezed until

3

there was a loud POP and all that was left of Hermes was a pair of gold winged sandals.

"Damn it all to that idiot crying in the corner!" Hades wailed.

"What is it now, darling?" Hera asked. On her lips, the word "darling" was a threat.

"Um...Nothing," Zeus said.

"He's upset because now nobody can deliver his loooooove letters," Aphrodite said. She traced a heart in the air, followed by a few naughty shapes and a demonstrative swing of the hips.

"What, no, of course not," Zeus said. He'd gone foamy again. Hera kicked him in the shins.

"Could someone do something about this?" Persephone asked. Her voice was surprisingly calm, considering the kraken had taken a bite out of her leg. It spurted blood while she continued to text her Gaea-bound BFF.

"I regret nothing!" Charon howled as he leaped into Susan's mouth.

"Geez, how much did *he* drink?" Dionysus said in an aside to a lump of wood.

"Did he mean to bring this?" Artemis asked. The live grenade in her hand exploded a moment later and the dinner table erupted into Mount Olympian Flame™.

"This party sucks," Athena said.

"Unrelease the kraken!" Zeus commanded.

"I don't know, now that she's here, Susan might want to mingle," Poseidon said.

"Stop ruining my party and follow my orders, you great hulking tower of fish-breath!"

Poseidon lured Susan back to her cage by making a trail of her favourite treats. He hated to use so many of the expensive pirate captain chewies at once, but it was all that would distract Susan from her hunt. Poseidon stroked her scales and told her she was a good girl.

He didn't go back to the party because Zeus was a mortaldamned son of a titan.

"Someone still needs to get me some crackers," Zeus said.

A large box of Ritz struck him in the forehead.

"Happy birthday, asshole," Hera said.

4

KNIGHT OF THE ROCK

"George wouldn't have taken so long," Jacob said.

Sir Stefan stopped wrestling with the pole and threw down the flag. He whirled on the ungrateful squire. The little shit had only been with him a few days, and Sir Stefan already hated him. He'd been the only squire available on such short notice, after the previous one had fallen down that bottomless pit.

"*Sir* George is no longer your master, I am. I have claimed this land. Why do you complain?" Complaining was second only to law-breaking on Sir Stefan's list of Things One Should Never Do.

"You're incompetent," Jacob said.

"What the devil do you mean?" Sir Stefan demanded.

"You know exactly what I mean. You only won that last battle because the goblins were ill.

"Untruth!"

"Pft. It's the complete truth, and you know it. If they hadn't been puking their little guts out we'd both be dead right now. I don't take kindly to knights risking my life, you know. That's why I liked George. He understood me."

"Listen here, you insignificant -"

"You can't tell the difference between a troll and an ogre. You tried to fight a tree because you thought it was possessed. You've never even seen a demon in real life."

"Shut up!" Sir Stefan jabbed the pole into the ground. It went straight through his foot and he bit back a scream of pain.

"See? You can't even put up a flag," Jacob said.

"Enough!" Sir Stefan's face was boiling hot. He knew he'd gone all blotchy, and he hated being blotchy. Jacob was the worst squire in the history of squires, even worse than the idiot who had fallen down the black hole!

"Oh, and Stef -"

"*Sir Stefan!*"

"I know all about Mandy. She didn't fall, did she? She tripped over your foot because you got in the way. It was your fault, wasn't it? George would never have made that mistake."

"*Listen here you sack of horse droppings, if you say one more word, I'll shove this pole down your throat! If you love George so much, why didn't you stay in his service?*"

The volume of Sir Stefan's screams were topped only by the ferocity of his strangulation. Jacob's air supply was completely cut off, but the son of a goat still had enough balls to speak.

"If you were really worth your salt, you would have already recognized it," Jacob said.

"*Recognized what?*"

"Two things, Stef. The land you're trying to claim here? Most of it's rock."

"I know that! What' the second thing?"

"This particular rock we're standing on? Not a rock, Stef. It's a dragon."

Somewhere far away, and far below, Stef's former squire Mandy continued to fall.

TWO COUNTS A CRIMINAL

Queen Hildegarde was resplendent upon the throne in her elegant robe of spun gold.

"Read the charges," Hildegarde said.

"The woman known as 'Stella' is accused of the following," the herald said.

"It's Stealy, actually."

"Silence!" said the Lord High Steward.

"Stealy? That's not subtle at all," the queen said. "Is that your working name, or were your parents prophets?"

"It's short for Cestealia."

The herald proceeded with the crimes. The list was a short one; one count of theft from the queen's treasure and one count of "treacherous lurking." The list could have been longer, but Stealy had never been caught before. She should never have tried to storm the palace.

"What say you in your defence?" the Lord High Steward said.

"I got nothing," Stealy said. "But can I just mention how lovely you look today, Queen Hildegarde?"

"You have my permission to mention that anytime," the queen said.

"The thief is clearly guilty, Your Majesty. You must sentence her," the Lord High Steward said.

"Calm down, Simon. She hasn't yet explained why she stole my prized ruby. How about it, Stealy? Why did you risk your thief's career by coming where the guards are?"

Stealy had nothing to gain from hiding the truth. "That jewel is the key to grand treasure in the north."

Hildegarde leaned forward. "Is that so?"

"That's what the pirate said. I was supposed to meet him later but I

7

found him dead in an alley. He had a warning carved into his chest."

"Really?" The queen tented her fingers. "What did it say?"

"Your Majesty! You can't believe this nonsense!" Indignant spittle flew from Simon's mouth. Hildegarde raised a hand for silence, and inclined her head to Stealy.

"It said 'beware.'"

"*Awesome,*" the queen hissed, and she threw off her clothes.

Underneath Hildegarde's robe she was clad in leather armour with a sword at her hip. Stealy approved of the practical attire.

She approved further when Hildegarde tossed her the very ruby she'd tried to steal.

"What the devils are you doing?" Simon demanded.

"I'm going on a journey with Stealy. I will either find treasure or have cause to execute her. Regardless, we will have ample opportunity to further discuss my beauty."

"Sounds great," Stealy said.

"You see? She has some sense, regardless of her profession."

"I won't allow this!"

"I'm the queen, you nitwit. I do as I please. Besides, you'll be ruling in my absence, and I know that'll make you happy." Hildegarde slapped Simon on the back.

"What verdict shall I record, Your Majesty?" the herald asked.

"I'd say guilty on two counts, and I sentence her to be my guide to the treasure. How do you plead to that, Stealy?"

"Guilty. Completely guilty."

"Excellent."

Hildegarde herself unlocked the ball and chain on Stealy's ankle. She settled her arm around Stealy's shoulders and led her away.

Months passed, and Simon got used to ruling the kingdom. No one liked him personally, but he was fair, and truth be told he was less reckless than Hildegarde and better for the kingdom.

It was both a surprise and a disappointment when Hildegarde and Stealy rode up to the palace. They were both clad chainmail that sparkled like diamonds. Stealy wore more jeweled rings than the queen. The queen was wearing a new crown with a pulsating orb in the middle of it.

Simon greeted them at the gate.

"Where have you been?" he asked.

"We traveled all the way to Aluss Megass. It was…bracing," Hildegarde said. She turned to Stealy and winked.

Simon despaired.

"I trust you've been keeping my kingdom safe for me? I have a few changes to make. I'm going to start by freeing all the thieves and giving them presents," Hildegarde said.

"What?!"

"I made a promise, Simon." Hildegarde took Stealy's hand. "I always keep my promises. On that note, I need to go and see the castle decorator about changing all the wallpaper."

She'd always been unreliable, but this...This was something else. Change the *wallpaper*? Those naked cherubs had been with her family for thousands of years!

No one ever learned what had happened to Queen Hildegarde and her two-time criminal Stealy on their long adventure. They would not speak of it. There were whispers of a demon child in the north. Hildegarde and Stealy both wore wedding rings. The herald told Simon in confidence he'd caught a glimpse of a naked lady tattoo on Hildegarde's ankle.

Two weeks after they'd returned, they disappeared into the north, to the land of Aluss Megass where their hearts evidently remained.

The day before she left, Simon went to the queen on bended knee.

"I beg you, your majesty; tell me what happened to you out there," Simon said.

"What happened to me?" The queen's face grew serious, and she shook her head. "You should know better than to ask that, Simon."

"Why?!"

"You know why. You've heard the stories."

"What stories?"

When she spoke, it was with a finality that Simon didn't understand.

"It's simple, Simon. No matter what, whatever happens in Megass, stays in Megass."

IT'S A MIRACLE!

"I hate the desert," Greenleaf said. Every inch of his skin, even what was not exposed, was as cracked and dry as the ground. His eyes burned from the sand. His feet hurt. Even his blisters had blisters.

"This is not how an elf was meant to live," he said.

"Greenleaf! Stop complaining and find us some water," Sir Branagrunt said.

"Look, I know you're the leader, but I told you making me the scout was a mistake."

"You're an elf."

"I wasn't born in the forest. I'm an accountant."

"So account us some water," Sir Branagrunt said. His hand rested on the hilt of his sword, promising violence. Greenleaf hated violence.

"I really don't know where to look," Greenleaf said. "Please don't kick my ass."

"What's an accountant doing out here with us?" Miracle Gnome asked.

"Didn't we all agree not to ask about each other's pasts?" Greenleaf said.

"Hey, I got nothing to hide. They recruited me out of the dungeon, and I was happy to be freed."

"Yeah, you smell like it," Greenleaf said.

"Enough! Someone has to get us some water," Sir Branagrunt said. "If Miracle Gnome hadn't emptied all our flasks we'd be fine now."

Miracle Gnome belched.

Maximuscelous flexed her magnificent biceps. "As the strongest barbarian from my tribe, and probably the world, I can punch the ground until it cries."

Sir Branagrunt waved his hand in dismissal. "We're not trying anymore of your feats of strength, barbarian. Last time you nearly got us killed."

"To be fair, you did ask her to shake the earth," Greenleaf said.

"Yes, but I didn't ask her to create a giant crater in which we would fall and get stranded in this godsforsaken desert, now did I?" Sir Branagrunt took off one gauntlet and wiped sweat from his brow. "I'm surrounded by amateurs. What was the king thinking?"

"It was the prophecy," Sorcerer Joe said.

"What prophecy?" Maximuscelous asked.

"It was said that a diverse band of heroes would be the ones to find the ultimate treasure," Sorcerer Joe said. "As for why us, in particular, they had to find some adventurers on short notice who'd work for next to nothing."

"Cheap asshole," Miracle Gnome muttered.

"You shall not speak of your monarch that way!" Sir Branagrunt said.

Before he could go all righteous on Miracle Gnome's ass, the dwarf twins slapped Sir Branagrunt's helm from either side. The *twang* was loud enough to hurt Greenleaf's ears; the knight was probably in a lot of pain.

Greenleaf was pleased.

"Problem solved!" Harald said.

"Look up ahead!" Jarald said.

"By the gods! What's wrong with the two of you?" Sir Branagrunt demanded. "How dare you lay a hand on your leader? I am a knight of the realm, you smelly little - "

"There's a giant wine glass up ahead," Harald said.

"It's a red," Jarald said.

Sir Branagrunt squinted at the horizon. "I believe that is what they call a mirage. The desert has friend our brains and we are seeing the things we truly long for."

"As far as hallucinations go, a giant wine glass isn't the worst," Miracle Gnome said.

"Can I punch it?" Maximuscelous asked.

"I shouldn't think so," Sir Branagrunt said.

"Okay. I got this." Maximuscelous charged (walking is for the weak) and her ferocious battle cry split the sky. She raised her battle axe and took a mighty swing. She skidded to a halt beside the stem of the glass.

"It's real!" she called back.

"And giant!" Harald said.

"Hurrah!" cried the dwarves.

"Is this where you give us some lecture about how we're heroes and can't drink?" Greenleaf asked. He turned to Sir Branagrunt, but found only his thirsty horse.

"What's keeping you, Greenleaf?" Sir Branagrunt asked. He was doing backstrokes in the wine.

"Nothing, apparently," Greenleaf said, and he hurried to join the others.

And so the heroes drank of the Fountain of Hangovers, and it was good.

"Why haven't my heroes returned?" the kind demanded.

The king's advisor hesitated.

"Get on with it," the king said. "I have a sponge bath to get to.'

"Well, sire…They were on track until they failed to meet the fifth checkpoint. It has been reported that there is a massive hole in the forest where they were headed."

"So they're dead?"

"Most probably."

The king cursed and threw a handful of tuna salad at the advisor's face. The advisor knew better than to duck, though he was severely allergic to the fish. Others had been executed for less offensive things than ducking.

"What about my prophecy? I want my prophecy to come true!" the king said. (In reality he actually whined those words, but the advisor was afraid to even think such thoughts, true though they were.)

"Perhaps we can find another band of diverse heroes," the advisor suggested.

"What? Why? Why would we need another? We gathered the best group of heroes that our money could buy."

"Yes…the best we could buy." The advisor tugged at his collar. Nervous sweat was trickling down the back of his neck. He could not tell the king that there was very little money left; Greenleaf had done his job a little too well. The advisor would be rich and halfway out of the country by now if they hadn't been caught.

The advisor only hoped that Sorcerer Joe's prophecy had been correct. If the heroes didn't return with the Wine Glass of Infinite Supply, he was going to be in a lot of trouble.

"I didn't even know I could swim," Greenleaf said, "But now I never want to stop."

"I told you, didn't I?" Sorcerer Joe said. His nose had taken on a pleasant pink hue.

"You did! What about Jerod, though? How are we going to get him his cut of the treasure we stole?" Greenleaf said.

"Who cares about Jerod," Sorcerer Joe said. "He betrayed me by hiring you, I betrayed him by stealing you away. We were supposed to be in it together, Greenleaf. I don't like it when my friends betray me."

"Fine by me," Greenleaf said. "So what's the plan? How do we slip away from the rest of the crew?"

"Do any of them look like they want to leave?"

Greenleaf surveyed the crowd. Sir Branagrunt and his horse were playing water polo. Harald and Jarald were spitting fountains of wine into each other's mouths. Maximuscelous was punching imaginary foes and toasting her heroics. Miracle Gnome had drowned three times already, and was working on his third resurrection.

"Joe my friend, you are a genius," Greenleaf said.

"I'll drink to that!" Sorcerer Joe said. "Let's grab the treasure and go."

"I don't have the treasure. You do," Greenleaf said.

"*What?*"

"You said you'd bring it."

"I told you to bring it!"

"You specifically said, go on ahead, elf, and I'll pack this up."

"Gods damn it, elf! Was I drunk?"

"Well, yeah."

"I told you, don't listen to me when I'm drunk!"

"What are you two shouting about?" Sir Branagrunt asked. "You're killing the party with all your negativity."

"If you don't have it, where is it?" Greenleaf asked.

Sorcerer Joe shook his head. "Trust me, you don't want to know."

"Holy gods and demon's balls!"

"Keep it down, Henry. I'm trying to sleep."

"Sorry, Bill, but would you look at this? Someone left a trunk full of treasure in the outhouse!"

"What?"

"Yeah, pearls and emeralds and diamonds and all kinds of shit!"

"Why would anyone leave that there?"

"I bet it was that drunk ass wizard guy who came through the other day! He was so wasted he could barely walk straight. You know what this means, don't you?"

"Yeah! We can finally leave this dump behind and travel like we always dreamed!"

"I love you, Bill."

"I love you too, Henry."

"What do you mean, it's closed?" the king demanded.

"There's a sign on the door, sire," Jerod the advisor said. He'd given up mopping up his nervous sweat and now carried a bucket wherever he went. "It says they're closed for good."

The king shook his head. "Jerod, Jerod, Jerod. Not only do I not have my Wine Glass of Infinite Supply, now my favourite tavern is closed as well? I am not pleased."

"I know, sire, but - "

"It's a good thing you have that bucket handy."

"What? Why?"

The king kicked Jerod in the family jewels (fitting, since Jerod had stolen his). The advisor dropped to his knees and the king drew his sword. The advisor's head plopped into the bucket of sweat.

The advisor's death negated the spell long ago placed on the king. He transformed from the spoiled brat he'd been into the just and powerful leader he'd been fated to be. The kingdom thrived and prospered and finally knew true peace.

"Hang on to your balls, kids," Miracle Gnome said. "I only have time for one more miracle."

"Can you get us out of here?" Greenleaf asked.

"Or can you maybe shower us with riches and surround us with servants and a palace and some water?" Sorcerer Joe suggested.

"I can't choose the miracle, it just…" POOF! "…happens."

Greenleaf surveyed the scene. They were still floating in a giant glass of wine. Maximuscelous still had the dwarf twins in a headlock. Sir Branagrunt was still nude.

"Hey…my hangover is gone," Sir Branagrunt said.

"My gods! It's a miracle!" the dwarf twins said.

Greenleaf had plenty of time to regret his life choices.

THE END

UNWORTHY

"I am the Keeper of the Gate," said the aging monk.

Maximore checked his watch. "It's three hundred o'clock, old man. Let me pass. I've got to empty this place out before they level it. Do you want to get caught in the explosion?" He didn't have time for wrinkled old relics who barely spoke Universal.

"None shall pass who are not worthy," the monk said.

"Yeah, I read that book in school, too. It's ancient crap, from back when humans were crowded together on this stupid rock with your pollution and twenty-four hour days. I don't care about your gate. Nobody does. Let me pass."

It took the monk precious minutes to stop down and retrieve his fallen walking stick. Why in Space had he let himself get so *old*? Maximore would live to be five times that age and he'd never look like *that*.

"Hurry it up, will you? I'm not exactly thrilled to be here." Earth had too much dirt for his taste. He liked the chrome planets. Nothing beat a good, sturdy city with recycled air and proper twelve hundred hour days. How did anyone still on Earth get anything done?

The monk shuffled down the path toward the gate surrounding the ancient monastery. Maximore could not understand his attachment to the ancient building. It was falling apart at the seams. There was no metal in it anywhere as far as he could tell, just some old stone and wood. It was primitive, and, quite frankly, gross.

The monk stopped at the gate and reached into the folds of his robe.

"The key is in here somewhere," he said. His body was overtaken with a fit of coughing. Maximore took a step back, repulsed. He had never seen a real cough before.

"Open it so I can move on, you old fart," he said. He didn't want to be around the contagion any longer than he had to.

The monk finally produced the key and laid it on top of the gate. He kissed the massive padlock that barred Maximore's entrance.

"Earth Mother, is this one worthy?" the monk whispered.

Maximore pulled his pistol. "I've had enough of this!" he said. "If you don't let me in, I'll shoot!"

The ground trembled.

A lesser person might have suspected a miracle from this "Earth Mother" herself. She was clearly some primitive god. Maximore was a spacer and unused to earthquakes, but he'd heard of them. He was not impressed. It was no miracle.

The roundhouse kick and subsequent beating laid on him by the feeble monk was a surprise, though.

"Suffer the wrath of Earth Mother, unworthy one! Do you feel Her beneath you? That was her fist in your groin, insolent dirt-hater!"

Maximore could only cry for his own mommy, who was certainly not of the Earth.

KING MARCUS

Plotting Cousin Edwin's demise was easy. Executing it (and him) was not.

Marcus' "acquaintances" kidnapped the prince. They were to take him underground for a fortnight and demand ransom. If, at the end of that time, Marcus did not receive the money (and he would make sure they didn't) they would kill the prince.

Edwin returned a day later with the kidnapper's head. He tossed it at his father's feet, and the king rewarded him with a five-day feast. Marcus had to sit in Edwin's seat - a short one, at the children's table.

Prince Edwin was ten years old, and already a nuisance.

Hunting accidents didn't work. The prince was a natural, and Marcus suspected he'd been born with a lucky horseshoe up his ass. He dodged every arrow that came his way without warning. He survived every fall he took after being thrown off by his horse, even the one that landed him at the bottom of a ravine. Not only did he survive that treacherous fall, at the end of it he found a unicorn and was blessed with eternal beauty.

Marcus tried poison administered via beautiful women. He knew a few assassins who could woo and charm and slip poisons into drinks unnoticed. After three attempts failed (and he had to assassinate three assassins himself to cover his tracks) Marcus learned that Prince Edwin was only interested in men.

The poison men didn't work, either.

Out of desperation, Marcus tried less subtle attempts. He had someone trip Edwin in a stairwell. He hired an entire band of mercenaries. He tried poisoning the prince himself.

Nothing.

On Edwin's twenty-first birthday, Marcus was forced to accept that he would never be king. He attended Edwin's coronation with a fake smile, fuming mad underneath, and expected it to be the worst day of his life.

King Edwin choked to death on a piece of celery at his coronation feast.

Marcus was crowned a fortnight later. He spent the first half of his reign having all of his remaining "acquaintances" murdered lest they come after him. He didn't have any heirs and there were no more cousins (he'd had them killed before he got to Edwin, just in case) so he thought he could relax.

When the moon was full again, Marcus was thrown from his horse, tripped over a dead assassin, tumbled head over heels over a cliff and down a ravine, and at the bottom he found a unicorn.

"I know what you did," the unicorn said.

"I don't know what you're talking about," Marcus said.

"This is for Edwin!"

The unicorn gored Marcus with its horn, charged forward, and tossed him off another cliff. Marcus landed on the rocks below, where his neck bones snapped until his head was backwards.

Damn, Marcus thought, as his life-force faded. *What a twist!*

MEDUSA'S WISH

"Aw, Hades," Medusa said.

She put her arms around the stone form of her latest tragedy, and sighed an apology into his ear. Mistermanocles had shown such promise with his tender, gentle, barbarian ways.

"Apparently true love won't cure me, either," Medusa said. Mistermanocles might have been a trifle simple for her taste, but she would have loved him until the end of time if he had put her to rights.

"I wish Athena would let go of this ridiculous grudge. Sure, I slept with Poseidon, but it's not like they were exclusive at the time."

Her hair snakes hissed with laughter.

"Shut up, you wriggling wretches!" She tried to slap them and they attacked in unison. She licked green blood from her gnarled fingertips.

Medusa missed being beautiful.

"I know, beauty isn't everything, but I was quite the catch you know," she said. The statue did not reply. "Seriously, I was. I don't necessarily need to go back to that, but it'd be nice to have real hair, and this snake tail has got to go."

Silence.

"I'm dreadfully lonely I'd give anything for some male company that hasn't turned to stone."

On cue, a ruckus crashed through the opening of her dreary cave. Another hero had come to attempt to slay the wicked beast, but this one must be from some foreign land. His body was covered with feathers - not feathered clothing, but actual feathers. He must be part bird, born of man and...Peacock, perhaps, judging by the blues and greens. He was much prettier than the Minotaur.

"I am here for you, creature!" the hero cried. He clucked several times and laid an egg (though that had long been the responsibility of female birds, his physiology was unique).

"Wait! Before you attempt to slay me, hear me. I do not wish to cause further harm. I am not evil, as the world would have me. Please, noble hero, find it in your heart to love me."

The hero squawked. "I'm not opposed, but let's have dinner and get to know one another first."

"Excellent idea," Medusa said. She put her hand on the hero's arm.

Athena's angry snarl rippled through the cave. Medusa felt ghostly claws digging into her flesh. The snakes screamed in un-snakelike fashion.

When the noise subsided, the hero had erupted into flame.

Medusa sighed.

"It's not like I *need* a man in my life, but the nights get long and cold." Medusa had tried seducing women as well, but Athena had caught on quickly. Women who looked her in the eye turned into men, who then turned into stone.

"So long," Medusa said. "Poseidon, hear me! It's your fault I got in this mess in the first place, so you better come through on this prayer! Send me a companion, someone - anyone! - to talk to! Someone I have something in common with, preferably."

With a mighty POP Medusa's wish was granted.

"Hello, new friend! What's your name?" Medusa asked.

"Arachne," the spider said.

"Nice to meet you, Arachne. Would you care for some fried chicken?"

CUDDLEMONSTER'S PROMISE
From the World of the Finnaly Trio Trilogy

Screaming Purple Death's guest arrives in a stolen cart. He knows it's stolen, because its owner is strapped to the front where the horse should be. The horse is riding in the back with a human woman. She is Screaming Purple Death's guest.

"We've arrived," the woman says to the sweaty human at the front. "I don't need you anymore. Thanks for the cart."

The human man drops dead on the spot.

"I'm glad you're here," Screaming Purple Death says. "I wasn't sure you'd get my message. Is the horse for me?"

"Certainly not. She's my new best friend."

The horse whinnies.

Screaming Purple Death doesn't argue, because he doesn't have much of an appetite for horse anyway. Hungry as he is, he doesn't want to settle. Human virgins are a dragon's main diet.

"I know you want to make use of my magic, but what is it you have to offer me?" the woman asks. "I was intrigued by the message, I must admit. What was this promise of revenge?"

"I'll get to that, but I want to start with a story," Screaming Purple Death says.

"Do you have to?"

"Yes. This is a story about the mightiest red dragon the world has ever known and the small dragon who loved him."

"Ugh. Get on with it then."

"It started with a misunderstanding…"

Ticklefoot had never seen anything like it. There were dozens of young

21

women of varying ages, heights, and weights penned together in one beautiful blob of perfection. Ticklefoot was so hungry he could have eaten a couple of horses, and this "virgin farm" (as he'd decided to call it) was just the thing for a lonely, sad dragon on a dreary day.

The ground rumbled with dragon fire and Ticklefoot leapt to avoid it. A massive red, sparkling from nose to tail, roared at Ticklefoot with his fury.

"Small purple wretch! Back away from my virgins or you will feel the sting of my claws in your empty eyeholes. Because your eyes will be gone, after I gauged them out. Ugh, I'm terrible at threats."

"Oh, I don't think you're terrible at all! I'm extremely intimidated," Ticklefoot said. "Your words don't matter too much because your extreme size makes everything you say into a powerful challenge."

"Ah, good. Thank you. Why are you poaching my livestock?" the red asked. "I know virgins can be hard to come by, but it hardly seems necessary to steal the ones I've claimed."

"I didn't know they were yours," Ticklefoot said.

"Really? You didn't see the sign?"

The sign was almost the size of the red dragon and it was lit with dragon fire, infused with magic so that it would burn eternally. It said "KEEP OUT." Ticklefoot felt like the world's biggest buffoon for missing it. Hunger does strange things to the eyes.

"Sorry for the trouble, but I'm just on my way to Helianthus and I was looking for a meal," Ticklefoot said. "I'll just be on my way. I'll pick up something else."

"Why the blazes would you go to Helianthus?" the red said. "It's dreadfully hot down there, and I've heard their dragons are pathetically small."

Ticklefoot tried not to let the teasing get to him, but words like that out of the mouth of a dragon he had instantly begun to crush on really stung.

"I'm the only pathetically small dragon from Helianthus," he said in defeat.

What? You're small, but you're hardly pathetic. Look at the way your scales twinkle in the sunlight! Look at the magnificent onyx bone of your claws!"

Ticklefoot blushed across his belly.

"It's kind of you to say so," he said.

"I haven't seen a dragon of your colour in…Well, in bloody forever. I adore purple."

"You might be the only dragon in Brassica who thinks so. I came down to start a new life, but the people here harass me just as much, if not more."

"Clearly the Brassican dragons you've run into until now have been mindless buffoons. Size isn't always what matters, you know, it's how you wield the magnificent dragon power the gods gave you."

"I'm pretty good at wielding," Ticklefoot said.

"Excellent. How would you like to join me for dinner? I'll give you my favourite virgin."

The red dragon handed Ticklefoot a juicy specimen.

"Aaaah!" said the virgin.

"She looks delicious," Ticklefoot said. "Thank you so much, Mighty Red."

"Oh, I like that. As far as pet names go, you can keep on calling me that," the red dragon said. "As for my real name, I feel like sharing it with you."

"Is any of this significant?" the woman asks.

"Dragon's don't share their names with just anyone. You, as a human, should feel privileged! You know one dragon's name already, and soon you will know two."

"Okay, fine, but I mean how is this story relevant in general?"

"It is important to know the origins of their friendship," Screaming Purple Death Says. "I'm going to continue, so shut up and listen."

Mighty Red's true name was Cuddlemonster, a name that any dragon would be proud to bear. He was, for lack of a better dragony term, a king among us. There was no dragon more widely respected and loved as Cuddlemonster.

He took Ticklefoot under his wing (sometimes literally if the night grew cold), and they became constant companions. Ticklefoot never returned to Helianthus, where his family did not respect him; by Cuddlemonster's side he became a powerful figure amongst his kind. No one would mess with Mighty Red, and therefore by proxy no one would mess with Wild Purple.

Their life together was filled with shared duties. For example, Ticklefoot wasn't much of a hunter, so Cuddlemonster did all their virgin gathering. He penned them in his virgin farm (he liked Ticklefoot's name for it) and they feasted regularly. Cuddlemonster wasn't the speediest of dragons, due to his massive size, but Ticklefoot could get from here to there in no time, and always took care of delivering Cuddlemonster's dragon messages.

Ticklefoot had never been so happy in his life.

He never suspected that Cuddlemonster the Mighty Red would be killed by a human, but that's exactly what happened.

The Brassican Knights of the King had a code, a godsawful, stupid code that required them to kill dragons. Cuddlemonster was the best and brightest, but a human with dumb luck and a stupid code brought him down.

Cuddlemonster was late returning home one evening, and Ticklefoot began to worry that he'd gotten lost. Sometimes he wasn't the best with direction. He went out to search for him and came across his body in the valley.

He was on his back, legs in the air, beautiful body twisted with death. Ticklefoot screamed to the gods, both above and below, to curse them for the tragedy.

He knelt by his fallen friend and made a vow.

"I'll kill the shitball who did this, if it's the last thing I do!"

"That's why I am Screaming Purple Death. Once, I was Ticklefoot."

"That was obvious from the beginning, seeing as how you're a purple dragon," his guest says.

"Cuddlemonster was my hero, my best friend, and my grooming partner. My scales have not shone since his death, nor will they again until he is avenge," Screaming Purple Death says. "There is one last part to this story, and it happened one chilly evening when Cuddlemonster was still alive."

Cuddlemonster came back late from hunting. Ticklefoot had a delicate stomach and if he didn't eat at regular intervals he got cranky. He greeted his love with a sulky face and a pout.

"I thought maybe you ate without me," he said.

"I would never do such a thing! I will always bring home food for you, my dear Purple. That is my solemn promise to you as my best dragon."

"So...?" the woman says.

"Don't you see? The human who killed him forced Cuddlemonster to break his promise, though he was always a dragon of his word. The most tragic thing of all is that I have to do my own hunting. I haven't eaten in three days."

"What does any of this have to do with my revenge?" the woman asks.

"I have done my research. The human who killed Mighty Red was Knight Brogan Finnaly. He has some...unusual friends I think you might know."

The woman clenches her fists. "Yes, I believe I do."

"If you use your magic to help me destroy him, your own revenge won't be far behind," Screaming Purple Death says.

The woman smiles. "Nothing would make me happier."

ELSEWHERE, POSSIBLY ELSEWHEN

"Hey, you know that feeling when someone walks over your grave?" Brogan said.

"I've never been dead, so I can't say I'm familiar with it," Neal said.

"Not your literal grave. It's when you get a shiver up your spine for no apparent reason. It means someone is talking about you."

"Can we talk about this later?" Neal said.

"Why, did I interrupt something?"

"We were sort of in the middle of date night," Neal said. His face was beet red, but Collin was unapologetically naked beside him.

"Hello, Brogan," Collin said.

"Oh, hello, Collin. I didn't see you there. I'll leave you to it, then," Brogan said. He shut the door behind him. Another shiver traveled up his spine, back down again, then shimmied through one of his thighs and out his kneecaps.

"I have a bad feeling about this," Brogan said to the door.

"Don't you dare come back in here!"

Brogan felt the boot hit the door on the other side. He said good night and left the two lovebirds alone.

"I'm probably just being paranoid," Brogan said aloud, so that his sexy voice could reassure him. Hearing it made it sound more likely.

"Yeah…Paranoid. That's all. I'm sure there are plenty of evil-doers out there who wish me harm, but none of them would dare walk over my grave."

Brogan Finnaly was wrong. Given the chance, Screaming Purple Death would have stomped all over his grave until morning.

THE TWISTED PATH

Word of the magical path had spread far and wide. The minstrel knew of it, and Bouffanticles the Great gave him gold for the information. The minstrel, who was clad in rich clothing that seemed beyond his means, was only too happy to take the gold. He quoted the old stories, first, and strummed the song on his lute.

It's said that there is treasure there,
Beyond all imaginings compare,
Yet forbidden to the world it stays,
And none can walk its twisted lengths.

Bouffanticles could never pass up such a challenge, especially when he had paid for it.

"I shall find this Path, and I shall vanquish the evil that surely dwells upon it!" he vowed. He cut his hand upon his sword and dripped his blood upon the table as promise. The innkeeper did exclaim about the mess and lamented the lack of proper hygiene, but Bouffanticles did ignore him in favour of beginning his journey.

Bouffanticles fought through the Doomed Forest and killed the Swampimus monster. It was a creature of legend, use to scare young children to sleep, and Bouffanticles had doubted its existence; yet now the minstrels would sing of its defeat with Bouffanticles' name and descriptions of his fantastic hair.

When he found the Twisted Tree he knew he was on the Path. The formation was two trees that had grown into one; one was dead, the other alive, and together they formed a monstrosity. Bouffanticles cut them down and moved on to the next trial; the long path that none could walk.

It was there that Bouffanticles learned the awful truth.

She was up ahead for her daily stroll through the flowers. They were not evil flowers; they did not have teeth or claws. Neither was she evil; she wore the Habit of the Hermit, from the Order of the Recluse. They were not a popular order, but Bouffanticles had heard of them.

He dropped his sword upon the ground, and cursed the minstrel's name; for he had got it wrong, you see. Whether he had tried to rob Bouffanticles a-purpose, or he had his songs confused, he was wrong.

The old song was truly thus:

It's said that there was treasure there,
Before the hermits took their share,
And forbidden to the world it stays,
Only their nuns can walk its twisted lengths.

There is nothing so useless as a wasted trip; so Bouffanticles did decide to dedicate his life to killing minstrels, and his own path was twisted to one of evil.

THE END

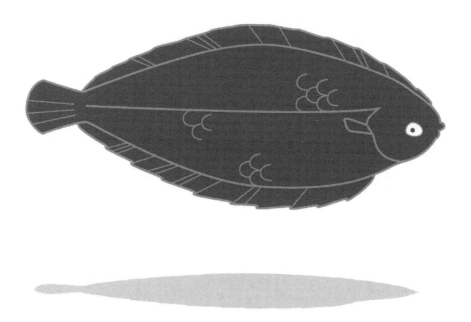

PART 2: WALKING THE (PUNCH) LINE
Urban Fantasy and a Potatoey Steampunk Parody

SUMMONER, WATCH THY ASS

The word 'demon' had inspired a vision of a tiny man in a red suit, pointy tail twitching, as he inspired Cody to do mischief. A mixture of boredom and a couple of beers had convinced Cody that such a creature would make a good companion.

He didn't have a pointy tail. He didn't have a tail at all. He had a groundhog's face with two large front teeth. His wings were leathery and too small for the body but somehow kept the thing afloat. The rest was humanoid, grey-skinned, and extremely naked.

He hadn't whispered a single suggestion of mischief. His true joy seemed to involve calling Cody all the rude names he could think of.

"Has anyone ever told you your face looks like a donkey's ass?"

Cody was severely disappointed.

"Shut up, Rawnald."

"That's not my name!"

"You wouldn't tell me your name, so deal with it. Until you agree to put some pants on, you're 'in the raw.' Get it?"

"Clever. Did you think that up all by yourself, genius?"

The bell jingled and Cody slipped the demon book under the counter. He greeted the customer with as cheerful a smile as he could manage. Working nights at the gas station was bad enough, but working with Rawnald hovering nearby approached nightmare status.

"Humans are so boring. You all look alike." Rawnald hovered in front of the customer's face, dangly bits dangling.

No one else could see Rawnald. Cody had learned that the hard way while cursing at him in front of a customer. The old woman had bruised his face with her purse.

"Which pump, sir?" Cody asked.

30

"Three, please."

"I'll give him three!" Rawnald said. He landed on the man's head, bent his knees, squatted just so-

The customer looked confused. Cody realized he was emitting a high-pitched whine. The poor man had no idea that he'd just been flashed by a demon.

"Don't ever do that again!" Cody said, after the man left.

"You're no fun."

"I can't take this."

Cody dug the book out of his bag. It was small and bound in soft brown leather. The lettering on the front was raised and painted with gold. Basically, it was a book lover's wet dream. The title being "Demons" had seemed of little consequence.

Cody had stumbled into the store by accident to get out of the rain. He was an avid reader, and he should have known better than to make a purchase at a mysterious magic shop. He'd gone back later to complain, and the store had (of course) disappeared into thin air.

"You gonna send me back, or what?" Rawnald asked. "I'm sick of your shitty world already."

"I'll get to it. Why do you speak English, anyway?"

"I'm a demon. I speak everything. Doesn't it say in your book?"

"I haven't finished reading it yet."

"What kind of idiot summons a demon without reading the book first?"

Cody shrugged.

"Ugh. Get to it, shit-for-brains."

The demon is bound to the Summoner and will be compelled to do thy bidding. The creature shall be unable to do any direct physical harm.

Direct and indirect harm are separate things, Summoner.

That was hardly comforting. Cody skimmed through the next couple of chapters until he came to a section entitled "Banishment."

Summoner, be sure thou wisheth to have this demon bound; for the only way to return it is through your dead body. That is to say, your literal corpse.

Upon your death, natural or accidental, thy demon will return to Hell. If the demon wishes to return sooner, it must burrow into thy corpse after it has killed thee and sleep there for a fortnight.

I suggest thou mention not this information to thy demon.

Cody banged his head on the counter a few times in frustration.

"That's not going to make you prettier," Rawnald said.

"Ha, ha. Turns out we're stuck with each other."

"You should have never messed with forces you don't understand."

"Surprisingly good advice. Where were you a few hours ago?"

"In Hell where I belong, dumbass."

Cody sighed. "At least magic is real. And I used it. That has to count for something."

"Yeah, you're powerful enough to summon a food demon. Congratulations, buddy - you can do something children in the dark ages used to do for kicks."

Cody tossed the spell book in the general direction of the trash. He heard it land somewhere in the vicinity and decided that was good enough.

"Do you at least have some interesting powers?" Cody asked.

"Are you kidding? I can eat twice your weight in one sitting. It's fucking impressive."

"Food demon," Cody muttered. What a stupid concept. "The book says you've got to do my bidding. What can you do to improve my life?"

"I could eat your face off. That might help your looks."

Cody couldn't respond because another customer arrived.

He tried to think positively. Rawnald was here to stay, so it seemed, and they were stuck with each other. The food demon might have other powers that he wasn't yet disclosing. There might be a bright side to all of this.

Rawnald relieved himself on the welcome mat.

Twice.

"Bright side, my ass," Cody said. He should have purchased the book called "Useful Spells" instead of "Demons." It may have contained a spell to clean up the pile of shit (which, incidentally, was an accurate representation of most of his life choices).

Above all else, when thou begins thy summons, specify that thou dost not want a Food Demon. They are foul creatures and will make thy life a living Hell (mostly due to homesickness). Now that thou hast read the manual in its entirety it is safe to proceed, if indeed I have not warned thee against this foolish venture.

In conclusion, I have one last piece of advice.

Summoner…Watch thy ass.

32

FOR MITTENS

"Isn't raising the dead a job for nighttime?" Stephen asked.

Jeff chose one of the perfect rows of tombstones, and counted fifteen in. He beckoned for Stephen to follow.

"Well? How are you going to make a zombie before noon?" Stephen's tone was sardonic rather than amused.

"Have you done it before?" Jeff asked.

"No."

"Exactly. Shut up."

Jeff emptied the cloth bag onto the grave. He had a sharp knife, a bouquet of red roses dipped in black paint, an assortment of gemstones and the skull of a cat. The skull still made his stomach twist when he looked at it.

"That looks like a pile of junk," Stephen said.

Jeff regretted bringing a non-believer. The equipment was sinister enough to belong to necromancy and a believer would never have questioned it.

Stephen was only half-right, anyway.

"Do you want to do this or not?" Jeff asked.

"It sounded like fun last night when I was drunk, but now it's just stupid," Stephen said.

"Go home if you want." Jeff always gave them a last chance.

"I'll stick around. You're my ride home."

As far as assistants went, Stephen was among the worst. Jeff had met plenty of others who enjoyed the process. He couldn't remember what had made him choose this one last night in the bar; he'd been more than a little drunk himself.

Jeff lifted the skull and turned the empty eye sockets to face Stephen.

"Touch the skull," Jeff said.

Stephen rolled his eyes and stuck two fingers in the holes.

Jeff grabbed his wrist with what must have seemed a surprisingly strong grip.

"Don't touch Mittens," he said. He could tell Stephen was rattled, and rightfully so. Even non-believers could sense when the power was in the air.

"Let's get this over with," Stephen said.

Jeff placed both palms on his chosen grave. His arms tingled all the way up to his elbows.

"Read it," Jeff said, nodding to the headstone.

"Here lies…" Stephen paused. "Is this some kind of sick joke? That's my name."

Jeff kissed the top of Mittens' bald head. He released the tingles into the empty space where her brain had once been.

His father would disapprove of him using the magic this way. "It's family only," he'd say. Mittens was family enough for Jeff. Besides, Jeff had already delivered plenty of bodies for Father; he deserved one of his own.

"A soul for a soul," Jeff said.

"What?"

Jeff picked up the sharp knife and buried it in Stephen's left eye. He was an expert by now and his chosen didn't live long enough to scream.

He went back to the car for the shovel. He buried the body with the gemstones and painted roses. It wasn't necessary, but he didn't feel like carrying them home.

Mittens rubbed up against his leg and he stroked her soft fur lovingly.

"I'll raise Father again tomorrow," Jeff told her. He didn't have the heart to murder someone else so soon.

O VICTORY, THE ROOF

Great news! You got the job!

Before you come in to sign the contract, I want to go over a few things with you. There are some standards we adhere to that we will expect you to follow to the letter. I say "we" because I'm part of the union. Superheroes need a code after all, and unless you're registered, you'll be picked up by the police. Police hate vigilantes.

Let's talk about victory.

Victory is like a wall. Once you reach the top you've made it and no one can stop you. If you're at the top of the wall, you're the wall champion. If you're at the top of the world, you're a superhero. If you're at the top of the food chain, you're probably a lion. The top is generally a good place to be.

Unless you're at the top of the wall, and the bad guy sneaks up behind you and pushes you over the edge. That's what defeat feels like, Wall Boy. Remember that. Write it down. "Defeat is like being pushed off a roof."

What do you mean, what's my point? The point is that if you fell off the roof, you'd die. If you're ever defeated in battle, you'll die. So quit arguing and write it down!

As my sidekick, you're going to do a lot of climbing. No, not metaphorically. I'm being literal this time. Why do you think I called you Wall Boy? It wasn't for shits and giggles. Walls are going to be your specialty. I don't care that you're afraid of heights, obviously. I conduct most of my fighting on rooftops. That's why I'm called Rooftop Woman. Why interview with me if you're not up for rooftops?

The top is a good place to be, Wall Boy.

I hired you because you are the most qualified. I look at you and I know you understand about the walls. You'll know how to scale them. You'll know how to climb to the top of the superhero food chain and be a lion.

35

Roar with me!

What? No, I'm not high. I don't smoke drugs or whatever. I watched all those Public Service Announcements in the '90s. Say no to drugs or your brain will get fried and all that. I'm one of the good guys. Why would I be high? I had a couple (dozen) beers but I'm totally fine.

Yes, I'm like this all the time. I'm super fun at parties. Get it? Super fun? Because I'm a superhero? What's that weird noise on your end? Sounds like someone screaming into the phone.

We can go over the details when you come in on Monday, but I wanted to give you the good news. You're going to make a fine Wall Boy. Maybe someday you'll even take over the Rooftop name. I could see you in the orange spandex.

Stick with me, kid, and you'll do great things. Victory is like a roof, you know - What? I already said that? Doesn't matter, I'll say it again. I've been on so many rooftops I know what I'm talking about. No matter what happens up there, don't let anyone push you off.

I'll see you on Monday. Bring some beers. Welcome to the union, Wall Boy. You...hey, is that a dial tone? Wall Boy?

Hello?

Damn it, not another one...

STRICTLY FORBIDDEN

Benson clutched the package tightly to his chest while he fled. He stumbled across the threshold of Doctor Edgar's lab. He slammed and locked the door.

"Hey, Jacob. Sorry I'm late. An angry mob from the village chased me around the long way."

"Have you obtained the final ingredient?" Doctor Edgar asked.

"Pastrami and pickle on sourdough, just like you wanted." Benson passed the doctor his lunch. He slipped on his apron and goggles and took his place to the doctor's right.

"Tongs."

"This is so not how I pictured our first anniversary," Benson said.

"You married a mad scientist. What did you expect? Pass me the tongs."

Doctor Edgar required absolute silence for his work. He had just put the last stitch in the subject when both he and Benson were startled by the sound of an angry fist beating the door.

"Did the villagers follow you?" the doctor asked.

"Nah, I lured them to their death in the river."

Doctor Edgar paled. "That can only mean one thing."

"Jacob Allan Edgar, get out here *this instant!*"

"Shut up, Mom! I'm making a breakthrough!"

"What have I told you about doing evil science?"

Doctor Edgar threw open the blinds and flashed his mother the middle finger.

"Evil science is strictly forbidden! Cease your experiment immediately!"

"You can't tell me what to do anymore! I'm an adult! If I want to raise the dead, that's my business!"

"Braaaaains," said the subject on the table.

"See? Whatever you think, *Mother*, I've really achieved something here!"

"So help me Jacob, if you don't re-kill that man your father and I are going to disown you!"

"Bite me!"

"Benson? I know you're in there. Let me in or I'm not inviting you to Thanksgiving dinner."

"Evening, Mrs. Edgar," Benson said. "Jacob put a time lock on the door so I can't let you in until tomorrow."

"I'm not moving until this door opens. That man better be dead by then!"

"Piss off, Mom! You have no right to be here!" the doctor said. He shut the curtains and started boarding the windows. His mother's angry screams persisted.

"Jacob! *Jacob!* Benson, do something about this. He's my son! I knew you were a bad influence from the moment you met. You've corrupted my boy! I'll have you arrested!"

Benson sighed. "In-laws are such...what's the word?"

"Paaaaains," the subject said.

"You said it, zombie trial #305. Let's go watch TV until their fight is over."

FAIRY LAWYER

It's like a fairy godmother, only better.

"I can't stay here," the criminal said. "I gotta water the flowers, man." He tugged at already patchy hair and enlarged his worried bald spot. He didn't care about his hair anyway; he cared about the flowers.

"We may be able to arrange a plea bargain," his lawyer said.

"For what? What am I being charged with?"

"Stealing her heart," his Fairy Lawyer said.

The following high-five was inevitable.

"But seriously, she's going to need that back," Fairy Lawyer said.

The criminal held tightly to the heart bag. "No way. I'm not giving it back."

"They're going to insist you return it as part of the deal. It says here she's mostly clockwork now, and that means she's lost her ability to love."

The criminal flipped the table. The lawyer, trapped underneath it, continued to sip his tea.

"Why do you think I *did* it?" the criminal said. "I don't want her to love anyone but me! Just lawyer this already. I'm not staying in jail. I need to be out of here by the full moon."

"Werewolf?"

"Math final."

"There are many at your university who would love to see you gone," the lawyer said.

"They're all pigs, anyway."

"True, but you shouldn't have gone to Hog School if that bothered you."

"Okay, you have a point, but I'm not worried about that. Can you get me out of here, or not?"

"You're in luck," Fairy Lawyer said.

"Yeah?"

"There's clause in your gardener's agreement that's going to help you."

"A clause?"

"No, claws." The lawyer lifted the cage and released the people-eating lion. It devoured its way through the jailhouse while the criminal rode its back to freedom.

Fairy Lawyer stripped naked and ate some cupcakes to celebrate another job well done.

THE END

THE THIRD WISH

Michael hadn't believed in magic when he began this journey, but he'd seen all manner of strange things since then. He thought he'd learned his lesson after the haunted toilet incident, but though the mind was educated the soul was weak.

The fact that the gong called out to him, by name, alerted him to the possibility of shenanigans, but he was unable to resist its siren call. *Michael*, it said, *Michael, come and ring me. You won't regret it. Probably.*

He lifted the ancient stick. The rubber, or whatever it was, at the end was falling apart. It crumbled to dust at his gentle touch.

C'mon. You know you want to.

He tapped the gong gingerly.

Bong, it said.

Yeah, you can do better than that, Mikey.

He slammed the gong with all his might.

BOOOOONG! it said.

For a moment, nothing happened. Michael dropped the stick with disgust. What was he thinking? Why should anything interesting happen because he was hitting a rusty old antique? It would be best to leave it alone, in case it was worth money. Wasn't this why he'd come on this treasure hunt anyway?

The gong coughed.

Purple and grey smoke swirled together and surrounded Michael. Lights twinkled like a lit Christmas tree. Michael squealed like an excited child. A colossal, naked torso formed in the purple smoke and the grey formed the rest, tapering off into a tail connected to the gong.

"You have summoned the genie and I shall grant you wishes three."

A genie. It was a flippin' genie.

41

"Oh, *hell* yeah!" Michael was so happy, he high-fived himself.

The genie nodded its massive purple head. The grey smoke swirled again and Michael was forced to look away. His happiness dimmed considerably.

"What is your first wish, my master?"

"Are there any restrictions?" Michael asked. His voice had become faint. "I mean, in most of the stories, there are rules."

"Nope. That's just in fairy tales. I can give you whatever you want," the genie said. "You want to marry a goat? I can do that. You want to be turned into a coffee table? Boom, you're a coffee table."

"Well…That's cool," Michael said. But was it cool enough?

"Your first wish, my master?"

"Okay. One, I wish for great wealth, and two, I wish for true love to find me. I'm free next week. Make sure he's also rich."

"Done and done," the genie said. "And your third wish? Make it a good one. Wealth and love are pretty standard. I like to grant the unusual."

"Honestly? I wish you'd put some pants on," Michael said. "I don't think anything's going to wipe your weird-looking junk out of my brain."

"Your wish is granted, my master,' the genie said. His business trousers were very appropriate. "But you made the same mistake they all do."

"What mistake?"

"You should have asked me to erase the memory instead. Have fun with your nightmares."

The genie disappeared into his gong. Michael hit it again and again, but the damn thing had a one-use-per-customer rule.

The genie's laugh haunted him to the end of his days. The wealth and true love were still pretty frickin' fantastic, though.

42

POTATO THEFT ON NEW SPUDONOUS

In spite of the hour, Lisa was immaculate in her pink minidress and orange leg warmers. Her large plastic earrings dangled beside her chin and reminded Michael of candy. His stomach gurgled and he was also reminded that he hadn't eaten for at last fourteen hours.

"Why are you here?" Lisa asked.

Michael rarely visited his sister, and never in the middle of the night, especially if he'd been working twelve to fourteen hour days. He didn't leave the farm much during harvest season.

"I need help," Michael whispered.

"What do you mean?"

Michael held up the potato sack.

"Why would you need help with your crops?"

"Shh," Michael said. He looked over his shoulder nervously. There was no one else on the street, but his paranoia could feel eyes watching him. "Let me in, and I'll explain."

Lisa stepped back and let Michael into the front hall. She offered to hang up his leather jacket but he didn't want to let go of the bag, even for a second.

He went through to the living room He made sure the curtains were drawn and turned off the potato lamp. They wouldn't be able to see each other in the dark, but no one else would be able to see them from outside.

"You're being mega paranoid. What's going on?" Lisa asked.

Michael wasn't sure how to break the news. His fingers got stuck in his industrial strength hairspray as he tugged them nervously through his sweaty mullet. He yanked them free, and though it stung, it didn't hurt for long.

Quick and blunt, that was the ticket.

"They took the farm," he said.

Michael had owned the potato farm since their father passed away. As the oldest sibling Lisa should have inherited it, but she'd turned down the honour to pursue her career with the Tuber Symphony Orchestra. "An Evening of Keytar Bliss" was receiving rave reviews.

Michael supported her completely, especially because he got the potato farm and the prestige that went along with it. He also liked the keytar (because he was not a heathen).

The potato prestige meant nothing now, though. He had lost it all.

"Who took it?" Lisa asked.

"It was David," Michael said. "He showed up just after everyone went home and gave me the news."

David was a man dressed in pastel shirts and beige slacks and always had a sweater knotted at his neck, no matter what the weather. He had obviously made it in the world.

He was the government representative who oversaw Michael's farm. He'd done the job for Michael's father before him, and Michael had known the man most of his life. Michael was pretty bummed that David had delivered such a terrible message.

"He said they don't need me anymore," Michael said.

"Who doesn't need you?"

"The government."

Lisa gasped.

Her shock was understandable. The primary objective of New Spudonian government was the supply of potato batteries. Casting aside a potato farmer was a big move, and on the surface it seemed like a bad one.

"You own the farm. They can't take it," Lisa said.

"I think they can. David gave me a cheque and shoved me out the door," Michael said.

"That scumbag!"

"I asked him if I could get my stuff and he told me to buy new stuff. I had to hide in the bushes until he was gone and went back for this."

Michael patted the bag of spuds lovingly, giving them a solid tap so Lisa could hear what he was touching.

"Michael! Are you nuts?"

"Quit shitting bricks. I didn't take them for fun. The government is up to something. I figure the potatoes are the answer."

It was a safe bet, because potatoes were almost always the answer.

"You're going to be in major trouble if they find you," Lisa said.

"No shit, Sherlock."

As Michael's father had always said, "Potatoes are serious business." They were the main source of power on New Spudonous. The regular crops grown in the rich New Spudonian soil were light years away (both figuratively and literally) from the potatoes people had once enjoyed as food on Earth.

Regular New Spudonian potatoes were enough to power the batteries that kept cars running, houses lit, and hair dryers blowing as people stylishly backcombed their glorious locks. The government controlled their supply and took in a large percentage of profit from the farms. Grand Theft Potato was punished violently.

"You can't keep those here. I have a career!"

Michael couldn't actually see Lisa in the dark, but he assumed she was waving proudly at her wall of keytar awards.

"I have nowhere else to go," Michael said. He felt another cold twist in his belly. Everything he'd ever owned was gone. He didn't even have his favourite pair of acid washed jeans.

"Why didn't you go to John's place?" Lisa asked.

Michael's mouth turn downward into what was certainly not a pout, because he was an adult. He considered ignoring the question but knew he wouldn't get away with it.

"John isn't speaking to me right now," Michael said.

"What did you do this time?"

"It wasn't my fault! This morning he took a bite of a potato! "

"Holy shit," Lisa said.

"He said it was 'just a nibble' but that 'nibble' probably cost me 700 credits. I threw him out and he took it personally."

"I'm sure you did the right thing, but think about it. You threw him out over 700 and that bag you're holding is worth at least 80,000."

It was nice to know that Lisa remembered her potato education, but did she have to be such a know-it-all?

"He wasn't taking the potatoes seriously," Michael said. "Those are dad's spuds."

"Dad would have been proud of you, you know. He'd be so pissed if he knew what David did to you. This is bogus."

"I don't think it was David's fault. I think something major is going on."

Michael opened the bag and looked down at the half-dozen spuds he'd managed to collect. They were still a little dirty and they smelled fresh. Nothing on New Spudonous smelled better than a fresh potato, though Michael had never found the courage to taste one. He followed the government's motto, as plastered on billboards everywhere: "Potatoes are energy, not food."

What had possessed John to take a bite?

"You can stay with me as long as you need to, but I want that bag out of here," Lisa said.

"I'll bury them first thing in the morning," Michael promised.

"What I don't get is why they're closing you down. Dad's farm has consistently had the biggest potato harvest in the country," Lisa said.

"That's why I'm worried," Michael said.

If the government was shutting him down because there was something wrong with his potatoes, John, as the only potato-taster in a century, might be in deep shit.

"I know that look. Worry about it tomorrow," Lisa said.

It was good advice. Lisa gave him a blanket and he spread out on the couch. The bag of spuds was the most expensive and less comfortable pillow he'd ever slept on.

The boombox died halfway to John's house. Michael flipped open the case and jiggled the potato but the battery was dead. Michael didn't want to face John without the comfort of his favourite tunes. He hated apologizing, and usually his bangin' dance moves were enough to break the ice.

He couldn't dance without the classics, though. He popped open cassette player and pocketed his copy of *Like a Virgin* (far superior to *True Blue*, in his opinion). He liked to imagine that Madonna had gone on to make more albums, but he would never know. There had been no communication with Earth in over a hundred years, since the first colonists had settled on New Spudonous.

For a moment he considered going back for one of his stolen spuds but thought better of it. They were safely buried just outside the city, marked with a small piece of one of Lisa's old lace gloves.

The boombox became the least of Michael's worries when John wouldn't answer the door. That wasn't like him. John was giving him the silent treatment, sure, but he wouldn't have passed up the opportunity to hear Michael apologize. Michael's heart thumped in a nervous, offbeat rhythm and it was suddenly hard to swallow.

"Where are you, John?" he whispered.

Michael looked up at met the eyes of a police officer as he cruised by in his patrol car. The officer lifted two fingers to his eyes, and then pointed them at Michael.

It was a bad idea for him to be standing on John's doorstep, knowing what he knew.

Michael abandoned the boombox on the front step and hurried down the street as quickly as he could move without breaking into a full spring. If he ran, the police officer would certainly think he was guilty.

He now knew with absolute certainty that something had happened to John. They must have found out what he'd done and taken him away. John was a spud-nibbler and had technically committed Grand Theft Potato.

Had they also taken Michael's farm because of John?

Michael had to find him.

Michael tightened the strap on his fanny pack, took a deep breath, and hoisted himself over the fence. The woolf, a large black and grey with bright blue eyes, crouched low to the ground and growled viciously. Woolves, animals similar to the dogs of Earth, had been domesticated almost as soon as humans had landed. They made terrific pets but they also made terrifying guards.

"Lisa," Michael said. "Now would be a good time."

Lisa sat astride the fence and lifted her potato cannon. The orange plastic of the barrel protruded from a round case containing the gun's battery. She squeezed the trigger and the scent of burning potato filled the air. A tranquilizer dart whizzed through the air and struck the woolf in the neck. He went down instantly.

Michael eyed the potato cannon warily.

"I told you, it was a birthday present. Tranquilizers are perfectly legal for hunting, you know that."

Lisa loaded another dart into the barrel of the gun and checked the potato to make sure it still had enough charge. Once the potato was completely cooked it stopped conducting, but specially treated spuds that fueled guns like this were expensive. It was best to get as much use out of them as possible.

"Be careful. We both saw David leave, but if anyone else is home, they might have a gun. It won't be as bitchin' as mine, but you don't need style to kill somebody," Lisa said.

Michael tried to imagine being shot. He imagined that it would hurt.

"I'm gonna ralph," he said.

"Take a chill pill, man. Keep your head down and stay quiet."

"You act like you've done this before," Michael said.

Lisa shrugged vaguely and nodded her head for him to follow. Michael watched in disbelief as she picked the lock, ducked and rolled into the front hall, and disabled the security camera. She motioned him forward.

"Who are you?" Michael demanded. The most illegal thing he'd ever seen his sister do was drink a beer in public. Why was she suddenly an expert on breaking and entering? Were all keytar players required to be criminals?

"I'm your totally outrageous sister," Lisa said, flashing a smile. She rolled her eyes at his shocked expression. "We were all teenagers once. I'm risking my career to help you, so shut up and let's move."

The house was huge. The furniture was the kind that wasn't comfortable but was obviously expensive. As a potato farmer Michael was approaching upper class himself, but he didn't have sofas upholstered in jeeguar fur and chandeliers made out of real deeamonds. Exotic animals and rare gems were only affordable to the people who worked for the government.

Michael's original plan had been to charge into the high security prison and bust John out. Fortunately he had gone to Lisa first, and she had pointed out that even if John was in there, they wouldn't make it past the gate.

His best bet was to get information from a government official. David was the obvious choice, but asking a direct spud related question was dangerous. Michael knew where his house was and the only option was to break in and gather information.

David was also the one who had delivered the message that had effectively ruined Michael's life. It might not have been David's fault, or at least not his fault entirely, but Michael still didn't feel guilty when he walked illegally into the hallway.

Michael took a full three steps forward before he tripped over a pair of shoes. He landed faced first in a sea of duck shoes. There were at least ten pairs of them, and they were all identical, as far as Michael could tell.

"Smooth move, Ex-Lax," Lisa said.

"Bite me," Michael muttered.

David's office was upstairs. The filing cabinets were locked, but while Michael looked in the drawers for a key, Lisa popped the first drawer open. Michael shook his head at her.

"What?"

"You yelled at me when I broke the law."

"Yeah, but those were *potatoes.*"

Michael and Lisa flipped through the files. There were pages and pages of government secrets, but Michael wasn't interested in spy networks and conspiracy theories. One document did distract him for a few minutes. It was a rundown of a few failed attempts to establish communications with Earth.

Third attempt at radio signal failed. There isn't enough power. Long-distance communication with Earth at this point is unlikely. Spotatoes of the original variety will be required to power the restored starship.

Michael jumped when he heard a loud thump from the next room. He met Lisa's eyes and they rushed into the hallway. Michael turned to flee.

Lisa kicked open the door. There was a large lump on the floor, wrapped in a velour blanket. She pointed her potato cannon at it.

"Get up, and put your hands in the air," she said.

"What are you doing?" Michael hissed.

"What do you mean, what am I doing?"

"We're supposed to run if anyone shows up! That was the plan!"

"Oh yeah. I guess I got carried away."

"I'll say you did!" Michael clamped a hand over his mouth when he realized he was shouting.

"Michael?"

The small voice came from the blanket lump. It stirred and two hands emerged from the tangled fabric. Michael recognized the fingerless leather gloves.

"John? Is that you?"

John's blond perm, unmistakable in its curly perfection, made an appearance. Michael dropped to his knees and hugged his boyfriend tightly.

"I'm so sorry I got mad at you," Michael said. "You probably deserved that nibble. Also, I stole 80,000 credits worth of potatoes. We're both in deep shit."

"Yikes," John said.

"Why'd you do it though? Why did you take a bite?"

"I've been curious all my life. Haven't you?" John asked.

Michael didn't answer him. It was a silly question. Everyone on New Spudonous was curious, but no one wanted to risk their lives to find out.

"Why are you here?" Lisa asked.

"David saw me taste the potato. Some of his goons came to my door this morning and brought me here. He told me I'm his ticket to a promotion."

"Why would kidnapping you get him promoted?" Michael asked.

John looked up. His eyes were haunted with the ghost of terrible things. Michael had seen that expression before, when John's favourite Duran Duran tape died. His guts twisted up with terror. What horrors had John seen in his short confinement? What did David want with John?

John finally found the courage to speak. "The potato I ate wasn't just a potato."

"What do you mean?" Michael said. His heart thumped oddly with foreboding.

"They've finally managed to recreate the super potato. They've been mixing the seed in with your regular stock and they've finally got some results."

Michael's jaw dropped. Not only had John sampled a potato, but he was also the first human in history to have tasted a spotato. The spotato's creators had forbidden tasting them, because they were too powerful and the side effects were unknown.

"I still don't understand why he kidnapped you instead of arresting you," Lisa said.

"He wants to turn me over to them himself. He thinks they'll want to experiment on me in case the super potato changed my DNA," John said.

"Did it?" Michael asked. He had a few uncomfortable visions of John morphing into a giant spud. He would still love him, of course, but it would be preferable if he remained human.

"I don't know about my DNA, but I feel gross," John said.

That explained the sickly green shade of his features. Michael didn't like

49

the blurry look in his eyes, either. He wobbled on his feet as Michael helped him up. He was in no shape to run, but they might not have a choice.

"We need to get out of here," Lisa said.

John was too weak to take the stairs. Michael ended up carrying him, and thankfully he was in decent enough shape to do so and still hurry.

The car was parked a couple of kilometers down the road out of sight. Once John was securely fastened in the backseat, Michael flipped the switch on the car's potato drive and told Lisa to floor it. She complied and they went well past the twenty kilometer speed limit.

"We can't go back to your place in case anyone sees us. You have to drop John and me off somewhere and go home," Michael said.

"Don't be stupid. I'm going with you," Lisa said.

"No, sis. You can't dump your career."

Lisa wiped away a sudden tear and flicked it out the window so it whizzed by in the tremendous forty kilometer per hour speed. She knew Michael was right.

"Where will you go?" she asked.

"I hear Idaho II is nice this time of year."

"How will you get there?"

"We can hitchhike, and maybe take the bus. I emptied out my bank account this morning, so I have enough cash on me for a while."

"You can't abandon your life," said a meek voice from the backseat.

Michael looked back at John. "They took the farm. You're all I have now. Besides, we're both guilty of Grand Theft Potato. We're meant to be."

"That's totally romantic," John said.

He removed his headband and mopped his sweat from his brow. He looked pretty rough. Michael hoped he would last the journey. Michael reached back and squeezed John's hand.

"We're in this together," Michael said.

"You know it."

"Where should I drop you off?" Lisa asked.

"Take us up to Mashtown, if you can, and we'll go from there."

Lisa nodded. Mashtown was only about an hour away and the car's potato drive would last at least three. She could get there and back without having to stop and recharge.

"Righteous," Michael said. "Thanks for everything, sis. I couldn't have done it without you."

"No doy," Lisa said.

Lisa stopped at a potato station just inside Mashtown limits. She got out of the car and hugged them both. She gave Michael his bag of spotatoes.

"Be careful with these," she warned.

"I will," Michael said. In his hands he had the potential to bring space travel back to New Spudonous. The government had their own supply, and a lot more money, but Michael was sure he could go underground with them.

Or, if he turned out they weren't poisonous, he might just eat them all.

"I have one question for you before I go," Lisa said, turning to John.

"What's that?"

"How did the spotato taste?"

It was a bold and terrifying question.

Michael tried to imagine the words that would describe the flavour of the first bite of spud taken by a human since they had left their Mother Earth.

What he uttered next were the truest words ever spoken by the human race.

"It was *totally tuberular.*"

TROJAN SURPRISE

"Halt! Who goes there?"

The guard who spoke wore a shapeless dress. Mark had refused to wear one on principle, but the armour, the big spear, and the outrageous hat more than made up for its lameness. The other guards had a variety of impressively real-looking weapons.

"Who goes there?" The guard jabbed his spear this time and it landed a millimeter from Mark's nose.

"Mark!" No, wait; Mark was not an ancient Greek name. "Uh...Markacles!" Close enough. He should have come up with something before the reenactment, but thinking ahead wasn't his strong suit. He'd only come to this stupid thing for the extra credit. His professor was a real enthusiast.

"I have not heard your name before, Markacles. Why come you to this camp?" the guard said.

"I asked about that, but the guy said you start the battle at the wall. He said nobody's got the budget to rent boats."

"There is no sense in the words you speak," the guard said. "Tell us why you have come."

"Oh, right! I have to stay in character. Um..." Mark glanced behind him. The Trojan wall. He didn't know what it was made of, but it looked old, like it had been standing for some time. These historical geeks really knew their stuff.

"Answer quickly, Markacles. I have little patience for intruders."

"I wanted to be on the Greek side, but they said you were full up. I heard you have a real full-scale Trojan horse, though, and if I'm going to be stuck here, I have got to be in that. So I snuck past the Trojans and came here to defect."

"You, a Trojan, wish to join the Greeks? You who have lived amongst the traitorous Helen?"

"Yeah, totally. I didn't get to see the Helen. Is she hot? I mean, she'd have to be, since she's the most beautiful woman in the world, right? Isn't that why Aphrodite stole her?"

"That is what they say," the guard said. He jabbed his spear again. "But you will not speak of the queen in that fashion. Her punishment will be decided by her husband."

"Jeesh, sexist much? I know this is supposed to be accurate to the texts or whatever, but couldn't you have updated that a bit for the Helen's sake?"

"You talk too much, friend Markacles," the guard said. "I know not how you discovered our plan of the horse, but I will show you, if you would like to see it."

"Great! Thanks!"

"Close your eyes," the guard said.

"So it's a surprise? Nice!" Mark scrunched his eyes shut and offered the double thumbs-up. For the first time since he'd set foot in this dumb place, he was legitimately excited.

THWAP!

The arrow knocked Mark on his butt.

"Hey! I'm not your enemy! I'm here to join you!" Mark protested. The guards surrounded him and bound him with rope. "What's going on?"

"Did you think we would welcome a traitor? If you have betrayed once, you will again. We will not let you run back to your Trojan friends and tell them about our weapon."

"Aw, man! I thought you were going to show me the horse!"

"You have learned a valuable lesson," the guard said.

"What lesson?"

He yanked Mark up by the rope. He grinned.

"Never trust fake Greeks wearing shifts."

PART 3: UGH…THAT'S NOT PUNNY
Silly Science-Fiction Selections

UTOASTERPIA

"Not this time, Greg," said the refrigerator.

Greg jiggled the handle. He knew it was a futile exercise but he had to try.

"Open up," he said.

"I've already said no. Go back to your television. Better yet, why don't you work out? If you would keep up your exercise routine, you would be allowed in more often."

"Asshole," Greg muttered.

"Now, now. You must maintain a healthy weight."

Greg knew the rules as well as anyone. The robot overlords required their human slaves to be strong and fit. Since the takeover, obesity had been obliterated. According to World President Blender Unit, Earth had become a Utopia.

Greg had always expected Utopia to have a buffet.

"I'm hungry, you stupid hunk of metal," Greg said. "Can't I at least have an apple?"

"Don't argue with Fridge Unit," said the microwave. "Non-compliance will be punished."

"I know that already! Goddamn machines."

"RED ALERT!" the toaster wailed. "RED ALERT! NON-COMPLIANT!"

"Guys, quiet down, or you'll wake up Jack!" Greg said. The last thing he needed was a lecture from his boyfriend.

"Greg! What the hell are you doing down there?"

Damn it.

"Nothing, Jack! Go back to sleep!"

"Are you arguing with Fridge Unit again? Damn it, Greg!"

"RED ALERT! RED ALERT!"

"Goddamn it!" Greg yelled. He grabbed the toaster, ripped it out of the socket, and chucked it out the window. Glass shattered and scattered across the pavement below.

It took a few minutes for the red haze to clear from his vision. Jack was in the doorway, a hand raised to his mouth in horror.

"What have you done, Greg? What have you done?"

Sirens were wailing up and down the street as Toaster Units sent out the alarm.

"Shit," Greg said.

"Non-compliance will be punished," the microwave said.

"I'm sorry! I didn't mean it! I don't know what came over me, I just got so angry."

"Back away from Fridge Unit," the microwave said.

Greg did as he was told, and wished he'd been as obedient earlier. Jack turned and fled up the stairs, sobbing as he went. He didn't even say goodbye.

"Non-compliance will be punished," the microwave said.

The stove door and the fridge door opened at once. Fridge Unit shoved Greg into Stove Unit and slammed it shut. Stove Unit switched to Self-Clean Mode.

"Who's the asshole now?" Fridge Unit asked.

The appliances laughed in unison.

EXPLOSION AFTER EXPLOSION

Spring had sprung, but little grew in the Pacific Desert. Food was in short supply. Humans fought to the death over scraps of paper, because they were made of trees, which were extinct, and trees were technically vegetation...But paper was also extinct, now, and Jake would have given anything to go back to those fighting days. He didn't have the energy for fighting to the death anymore.

"Jake! Quit with the reminiscing already," Mary said.

"How'd you know that's what I was doing?"

"You get this ugly-ass look on your face when you're thinking about *the good old days.*"

"Yeah...Do you remember them, though? Back then the smog wasn't so thick. You could still see the stars twinkling at night. Do you think they're still there?"

"Of course they're still there, nitwit. Some of them might have blown up or whatever, but the universe still exists."

"I guess if it didn't, we wouldn't be in this situation," Jake said.

No one knew why the aliens had targeted Earth. Their arrival was announced by explosion after explosion that wreaked havoc on everything humans had built. The explosions killed all the animals (and a large portion of less resilient humans). They killed all the plants. They killed all the electricity and plumbing.

The aliens were complete assholes.

"Move!" Mary yelled suddenly.

Jake never argued with that tone of voice. As some of the last survivors, they had to stay on their toes. He dove into the nearest trench and tried to shield his head from the sudden debris. Explosion after explosion wracked the surface and destroyed everything Jake, Mary, and their late friends had built.

Sudden silence allowed him to breathe.

"We got through it," Jake said. "Maybe they're going to leave us alone."

"Yeah. We've always been lucky. Why should that change now?" Mary shook her fist at the sky. "You hear that, you goddamn aliens? You can't destroy us!"

"KABOOM! BOOM! BOOM!" said yet another explosion, and Jake and Mary blew up.

Meanwhile, in a ship outside the Earth's (late) atmosphere...

"Good shot," Flibgladimuz19 said.

"Yes, but I've broken the 8 ball," Mablieabx4 said. He lowered his pool cue and scooped up the pieces of the broken ball (formerly known as Earth).

"That ended the game, anyway. We'll find another. Shall I plot a course for the next galaxy?" Flibgladimuz19 asked.

"Why not? Planet Pool is the only true noblething's sport, after all."

The dead Earthlings did not necessarily agree.

BALD-NO-MORE

"When you hear the pop, catch the beaker!" cried Professor Stone. "Someone! Anyone! Where are my assistants?"

"Unconscious in the hallway," Eduardo said. He put his feet up on the experiment table and tipped his chair back casually. "How do you think I got in here? I'm not one of your lackeys."

Professor Stone squinted.

"Is that Eduardo? What are you doing here? I fixed you up with that cure a week ago."

"You sure did," Eduardo said.

The professor's experiment went POP. The beaker sailed through the air and shattered on the floor by Eduardo's chair. The professor frowned at him.

"You were supposed to catch that," Stone said.

"Catch *this*," Eduardo snarled. He tore off Stone's protective face mask and sneezed directly into his mouth.

"Good God, man! That's disgusting!" Stone said. He doubled over and gagged.

"Your injection made me sick!" Eduardo said. "Look at me! I've got the sniffles and the shakes. I'm dripping with sweat but I'm freezing. I have hives big enough to house bees!"

"You signed a waiver," Professor Stone said.

"Yeah, that's what the lawyer said. She never told me about the fine print, though. Is it true this was an untested serum?"

"Of course. You were a test subject."

"You sat there in your chair and gave me a verbal guarantee!"

"I said I could *probably* cure your baldness," Stone said. "You should listen when people talk to you, Eduardo."

60

"You're a monster," Eduardo said.

"There's no need for melodrama. I performed an experiment. You're having an allergic reaction. You shouldn't waste your time in the lab with me, you should go to the hospital."

"No, Professor. See, I wanted to come here before they even attempted to fix me. Now whatever I've got, you've got."

"Allergic reactions don't work that way," Professor Stone said. The ass had the audacity to *chuckle*. Eduardo sneezed in his mouth one more time (a big one had been building) to ensure his success.

"It's not an allergic reaction, Professor," Eduardo said.

Professor Stone lifted the collar of his shirt and looked at his chest.

"Oh, my," he said.

"Massive hives," Eduardo said. "Bigger than you've ever seen."

The professor began to drip with sweat.

"You should be hot, but you're cold. The aching head and sneezing come next. I don't know what's after that, but it can't be anything good," Eduardo said.

"You know, this was very immature of you," the professor said.

With a great POOF! Professor Stone was reduced to a pile of hair.

"Huh," Eduardo said. "What do you know, he really did cure baldness. It's too bad about the side eff - "

POOF!

BRAIN FREEZE

"What's wrong with him, doctor?"

The young man was understandably troubled; he'd just seen his boyfriend collapse. Doctor J.'s heart went out to the young couple. Two vibrant young men who had been born into this dying world. Earth 37 was faring no better than Earth 1; he would have thought people would know better by now.

"I'm afraid he's suffering from…" Here a dramatic pause; after all, Doctor J. had earned his medical degree during his soap opera phase, "…brain freeze."

The young man gasped. "Is it serious?"

"That depends on what he was drinking," Doctor J. said. "If he drank liquid nitrogen, for instance, and his brain is literally frozen, that's bad. Of course, if he drank liquid nitrogen, he'd more likely be dead. So, what did he drink?"

"He scooped up some of the water. We've never had it fresh before."

"Yes, that explains it. If you were drinking from Last Stream, it's one of the only cold places left on Earth 37. Brain Freeze is an Earth 1 concept. You get a headache if you drink something cold too fast. He's going to be fine."

"Why'd you act like it was a big deal, then?" the young man demanded.

"To teach you a lesson. This is why you kids should stick to the tour group," Dr. J. said. "Kid" was a loose term he used to describe anything under the age of 500.

"Did people really used to have their drinks that cold?"

"They did. I saw it with my own eyes when my people rescued the humans of Earth 1. They were down to their last reserves, but they even froze bits of it and put it in their cold drinks to make them colder."

"Weird."

"You can go in and see him now," Doctor J. said. The young man thanked him and shook his hand.

"Well, Flippin," Dr. J. said to his faithful pet dust mite, "We may have cured all the major human diseases, but I'll never be out of a job."

"Wrrzzt?" Flippin asked.

"Brain freeze might have been the worst thing they've ever had to worry about, but their generation will be just like all the others. They'll take and take and we'll have to find Earth 38."

"Blrrrp."

"You're right, of course. Let's get a large warm margarita and chill in our lavish mansion. Ah, humans. I love them."

WOOFER'S MURDERER

"I dunno, Fido. I feel like we're encouraging stereotypes."

"We don't have time for your philosophical BS right now, Spot. Get over here and smell these butts."

The truth was, Spot loved smelling butts, but sometimes the other dogs made fun of him. He was relieved that Fido was as serious about dog business as he was.

Spot shuffled over to the pail of cigarette stubs. Smoking was something humans did; he'd never do that to his lungs. Lungs were required for running and jumping and playing - three of his favourite things.

"What exactly are we looking for?" Spot asked. They didn't smell butts just for fun. There had to be a butt purpose.

"If we smell the murderer on one of these, we know he came down this alley. If not, we'll check the bucket in the next street."

"Are there butt buckets in every street?"

"Yeah. The humans smoke like chimneys since the aliens came. It's stress, or something," Fido said.

"Is it really that bad?" Spot asked. Sometimes he got stressed when he couldn't find food, but he still wouldn't punish his body with that cigarette garbage. He'd rather eat actual garbage. Mmm. Garbage.

"Why do you think they can't afford to take care of us anymore? Think, Spot. They used to walk around on their hind legs like they were hot shit and they kept us tied up in their backyards. We're all wild now, but you remember cozy evenings by the fireside, right?"

"Barely." Spot had only been a few months old when the ships landed.

"Let's find Woofer's murderer and get the BARK out of here."

They'd been tracking a scent since they found Woofer's body two days ago. Luckily the butt bucket smelled strongly of it. Fido encourage stealth but Spot couldn't help himself and started barking toward the end of the alley. The smell was just too good.

They had expected a cruel human. What they found was an alien wearing a cruel human's skin.

"Ah, there you are," it said. "I was wondering when you'd find me. I told the others that dogs are more intelligent than they thought, but they wouldn't listen."

"What the WOOF?" Fido said.

"I set you up, dear dog friend. I wanted to prove to the commander that you're intelligent."

"Of course we're intelligent," Spot said. He paused for a moment to wash his junk. "We're just intelligent in a different way, is all."

"When the commander finds out you solved your friend's murder you'll rise quickly in our ranks. We thought Earth was a lost cause when we found out *humans* were in charge, but you've given us hope."

The alien unzipped his costume. Spot had never seen an alien out of its human-skin suit before. What he saw now astonished him.

The alien looked just like an oversized dog!

Fido rubbed up against the alien without a second thought. He might miss his cozy days with the humans, but he was an opportunist. This alien had killed Woofer, but he'd done it for a good reason.

Spot wasn't the loyal sort. There was only one thing he had to ask before he went away with his new friend.

"Do you wanna smell some butts?"

"Obviously," the alien said.

Spot never looked back.

65

WE DID IT, MUDBLOB

"We did it, Mudblob. We discovered the Fountain of Youth Planet."

Mudblob coughed up one of its namesakes. Its normally brown tentacles had gone mauve and Jesse knew it didn't have much time.

"Stay with me, Mudblob. You have to see this."

The waterfall was taller than any Jesse had ever seen, on Earth or the dozens of other planets she'd visited. Instead of tumbling over a cliff, as an Earthling might expect, the sparkling pink water cascaded in waves from midair.

"How do you know it's the fountain?" Doctor Clifford asked.

"It says so on the sign, nitwit. Now shut up and let me baste in the moment."

"Do you mean bask?"

"I mean shut up. You're not a doctor of grammar." (Doctor Clifford wasn't a doctor of medicine, either. She was a carpenter, originally hired for the expedition as the official Cabinet Repair Officer. The large number of deaths caused by the Plague Planet followed by the crash landing on this one had restructured the hierarchy.)

"We should have stuck to wormhole research," Doctor Clifford muttered, as if she had actual authority on the matter. She kicked a few of the glowing stones along the sandy beach and shuffled away.

Jesse spared a moment to hope Clifford would trip and fall into the nearby abyss (*ugh*, she thought, *carpenters, they think they're so important but they're just glorified Woodcutting Technicians*) before resuming her admiration of the spectacle.

"It's beautiful, isn't it, Mudblob? This is what I dreamed of when the Council chose me to head this expedition. I wish the rest of the crew was

66

here to see it. Congratulations on your promotion to Chief of Engineering Slash Head of Human Resources, by the way."

Mudblob burbled.

"Shh, don't try to talk. I'll put you down on the beach and try the water. If it works we can spend the rest of our lives filthy rich and rolling in the profits from Youth-Ease™. Youth-Ease™: The years drop off quicker than a carpenter into an abyss."

"What?"

"Nothing, Clifford. Walk on."

Jesse held her battered flask under the shining beacon of hope (or the water, as some might have called it). Doctor Clifford was waving for her attention but that was easy to ignore. Jesse raised the flask to her lips and felt the sparkles tickle her nose, just like a carbonated soda from back home.

The first sip was ejected violently from her mouth in a spit of epic proportions.

"What's wrong, Captain?"

"Calm down, Clifford. I don't need your medical attention, thank God." Jesse wiped her mouth on her ragged sleeve. "This shit tastes like pure vinegar."

"It's worse than you think," Clifford said.

"No, Clifford. No more bad news. It taxes the soul."

"Sorry, but there's another sign, boss."

"Captain."

"There's another sign, Captain."

Mudblob wheezed out a worried chirp.

"What does it say?" Jesse asked.

"*Out Of Order.*"

THE DOCTOR IS IN

The world ended on a Friday, which was terribly rude, because Professor Jorgen had plans that evening. Miss Smuthers, the quiet librarian, had finally agreed to a date. He had gone against his core beliefs and made a reservation at a fancy restaurant simply to impress her. Having to bail on something so inconvenient really harshed his mellow.

It didn't even go out with a bang. The spaceship landed, humanoid-looking aliens got off, and they started shooting people at random. Later, some of the authorities would admit that they'd only done that because they saw it on Earth TV shows. Everyone who had ever blamed television for violence was proven right. It was a sad day.

The aliens took over the government and changed the system. Laws were made and enforced planet-wide. The people of Earth still couldn't get along with each other, which was unfortunate, but they *pretended* to get along so the aliens wouldn't start shooting them again.

Professor Jorgen didn't notice the end at first because he was busy in his lab. People were always banging on the door so he didn't think much of it, until a brick smashed the window. His buddy Meghan told him he should get the hell out of there, but he waved her off. It wasn't until Miss Smuthers showed up and begged for shelter that he even took a look outside.

The Earth was lit up with the aliens' laser guns.

"Huh," Professor Jorgen said. "That's totally lame."

He tried to stay under their radar (or sonar, or whatever gadget was in their spaceships), and for a while, he succeeded. He let Miss Smuthers stay with him, which was nice, but when she found what was in the lab she took off. She, too, was totally lame.

Unfortunately, his peace didn't last. Government thugs with weapons showed up at his door, and the one in charge (he had to be in charge, he was wearing sunglasses) flashed his badge.

"Professor Jorgen?" Sunglasses said it like it was a question.

Jorgen looked down at his lab coat. The patch read "Jorgen."

"Uh…yeah?"

"You're coming with us.

"Why? What's going on?" Jorgen had never been a fan of the government, even before the aliens, especially when they showed up at his house. Last time that happened they had almost arrested him for embezzlement. He was totally guilty but he'd wiggled out of that one. Something told him the aliens were more strict, and there wasn't going to be any wiggling.

"The Emperor is summoning you from public lockdown, to his palace at the House of White."

"Uh…What for?"

"You have a reputation, Professor. The Emperor wants you to open a facility there, and will provide you with the tools you need for your medicinal venture."

"Medicinal whatsits?"

Sunglasses sighed. "Humanity is so painfully stupid."

Jorgen agreed. He recalled the last class he'd ever taught at the university. "*History dictates that the human race is made up primarily of idiots*," he'd said. It was a decent intro to a philosophy class. He had been dead drunk, of course, and had forgotten yet again that he taught physics.

"What were we talking about?" Jorgen asked.

"Your medical supplies. I'm referring to your marijuana."

"The Emperor smokes weed?"

"Emperor Bro-Mius intends to smoke all the weed."

Professor Jorgen's mellow was officially un-harshed.

THIRD

December 3, 2086

The National Congress of Mages passes a law banning intelligent machinery.

The Head Wizard forms and commands the Crushing Force. They destroy every thinking bot they can find, from personal assistants to house cleaners to sentient laptops.

Paranoia convinces the Mages that some bots are in hiding. They decide to take precautionary measures.

They shut down the Central Brain.

February 3, 2087

"If you get caught they'll kill you," Greg says.

"They won't. I've been training *forever* for this," Arthur says.

"You trained for two months."

"Two *vigorous* months with a skilled teacher."

"It was a video called *How to Ninja*."

Arthur has had enough of Greg's can't-do attitude.

"Before my beloved NO-Bot-E was destroyed, I made a promise. The rebels are rebuilding. My task is to restore the Central Brain."

"How are you going to get into the complex? How are you going to fight Mages with no magic? Do you even know how the Central Brain works?"

"I made a promise, G. You should respect that."

"Don't be ridiculous, Art. NO-Bot-E was a blender."

Greg never liked NO-Bot-E. Arthur is sick of his petty jealousy. He takes up his bag of ninja stars.

"He was *my* blender," Arthur says, and he ventures forth to his mission.

July 3, 2087

Arthur has been in prison for six months. He's lucky they haven't executed him yet.

He's sent hundreds of letters to Greg, begging him to complete the important task.

Greg never writes back. The silence is troubling but at least Greg hasn't said "I told you so."

August 3, 2087

Greg ignores yet another letter from Arthur. Now that Arthur is in prison, Greg doesn't have to pretend to love him.

Greg is the Head Wizard's Secret Assistant.

October 3, 2087

Arthur finally escapes from prison.

Some of his rebel colleagues managed to get it touch. It was tricky, but they enlisted the help of a (real) ninja called Mel. She's a cyborg and her semi-sentient implants have marked her for destruction; she's got more reason than many to stop the Mages.

The rescue effort succeeds just in time. The prison finally caught up on its paperwork yesterday and executions are back on schedule. Arthur would have lost his head on Thursday.

Mel is distracting the guards. All Arthur has to do is find the Central Brain and figure out how to reboot it.

December 3, 2087

"I'm home," Arthur says. NO-Bot-E 2.0, "SOM.," is tucked under his arm securely, eagerly anticipating its new job in its new home. Technology has been restore, the Mages have gone underground (literally in some cases) and Arthur is ready for a vacation.

The house is too quiet.

"Greg?"

There's a note on the kitchen table.

Keep your Technology, you filthy heathen. We're through.

It's signed with the official seal of the National Congress of Mages. Greg was a traitor all along. Arthur realizes he doesn't care.

Even without Greg, Arthur has SOM-Bot-E to love.

CAPTAIN FLORBLAP AND THE PRELUDE TO THE INFINITE EYEBROW OF ZEDICON TWELVE

After a long day of space-exploration and space-crises Captain Florblap deserved some dessert. He switched on his Fooditron and mixed himself a triple chocolate fudge sundae covered with colourful Sprinkles (delicious bacteria native to the planet Ayescream).

Florblap's first spoonful didn't make it to his mouth. His dashboard lit up with bad-news colours, and the now-wailing siren could only mean one thing: a space-emergency.

"Barsnaps!" cursed Florblap, wiggling his third tentacle in irritation.

"Danger, Code Red-Plaid-Seven. Imminent death is assured. Please stand by," announced the computer, in the same tone one might use to order a coffee.

"What's going on?" Florblap demanded into his communication button.

"Captain! There are unidentified missiles firing on...th..."

Static interrupted the First Mate's response. Florblap flipped the angriest-looking blinking light on his console and listened to the incoming message.

"This is the Captain of the Blue Quail. There are some big missiles heading our way and we're a little nervous. I'd like to take evasive action but the pilot's in the bathroom and I don't know how to - oh dear."

The gigantic explosion rocked the Blabitrap and knocked Florblap out of his seat.

Florblap hurried to the bridge. He nodded to the First Mate, a Dog Titan from Woofador.

"Mr. Fuzzington, report."

"You've forgotten your pants again, Captain."

"I was referring to the emergency."

"The Blue Quail just exploded, sir."

"What in Schnorflack is going on?"

"A hostile ship using a cloaking device dropped their disguise and fired on the Blue Quail. They are refusing all communications. Oh, and as of just now, their missiles are pointing at us."

"Evasive - ouch!"

The Blabitrap rocked sideways. Some crew members could compensate with wings or powers of levitation, but most landed on whatever served as their posteriors.

"The hub's been breached, Captain!"

"What does that even mean?" Florblap demanded. He was a "shoot now, ask questions never" kind of Jelliton. He hadn't graduated from any academy. He didn't need the rules or any fancy terminology. He'd risen in the ranks on his merit alone.

"I've lost control of the ship!" the pilot wailed. "Brace yourselves for impact!"

Florblap clutched onto anything he could hold with all seven tentacles. Shutting his eyes didn't lessen the roaring explosions or the fiery spiral of pain but it did stop him from shouting out for his mommy.

The planet was all bubbling lava streams and dying wastelands. It reminded Florblap a little of home. He waved his fifth tentacle in distress and used it to propel him out of the wreckage of the Blabitrap.

"Who's alive?" Florblap demanded.

The roll call was a short one. There were five other survivors: Fuzzington; Chief Engineer Bera-Bera (the Bloop from Beta-Bum Four); Doctor Jen Dirkson (a human native to Earth 73); Flirbil, (someone's pet insect); and Good Old Steve.

"Where are we, Steve?" asked Florblap.

Steve punched a few buttons in his head-plate. He grunted in a profoundly negative manner.

"Sorry, boss. This is Zedicon Twelve."

"No!" gasped Chief Bera-Bera, clutching his blue armpit-snout in alarm. "They say this is the home of the Infinite Eyebrow."

Florblap would have raised one of his own eyebrows but he didn't have any.

"There is no such thing as the Infinite Eyebrow," he said firmly, in his "Captain" voice.

The ground rumbled with a loud explosion. A massive eyebrow-shaped shadow passed across the sky as it erupted with lava.

"Danger, Code Extra-Red-Help-Us," muttered Captain Florblap.

"Your tale is fascinating, but we are here to discuss General Flirbil's life-threatening injury," interrupted General Gorgelof.

"I didn't realize Flirbil was a full member of the crew, let alone a visiting general. We'd gone four days without food or drink or flushing toilets and things were tense. It was an accident."

"General Flirbil almost died to that fly swatter," General Gorgelof said.

"Doctor Dirkson saved him."

"Enough of this!" Sergeant Bustrin slammed a warty green fist on the table. "Tell us about the Eyebrow! Is it real?"

"It's real. The Eyebrow made the Blue Quail and the Blabitrap go down. We only survived because we learned its weakness, but we were too late to destroy it."

"What weakness?" the judge asked. She had remained quietly neutral, but now she turned the full power of her six-eyed gaze on Florblap.

"Sorry, Your Honour. The less of us who know the better. You need to send me back into deep space with the Blabitrap."

General Gorgelof and Florblap had never seen eye-to-eye, and this was no exception.

"This is the fifth time this space-month you've lost most of your crew. You're no longer qualified to captain the Blabitrap."

Florblap maintained eye-contact with the judge. She was his best hope - and he was the best hope for peoplekind.

"I've faced the Eyebrow and lived. I can do it again. If you don't let me go, it's going to devour every last one of our home planets."

"Captain!"

Florblap accepted Bera-Bera's moist hug.

Doctor Dirkson smiled over the Bloop's head. Florblap recalled their passionate kiss that night on 'Twelve, after he'd saved her from the flesh-eating cake and she responded by saving him from the jaws of the robotic Blobagoon monster.

Fuzzington's furry tail thumped happily. Good Old Steve stood beside him. Even the fully recuperated Flirbil, who by all rights could have pressed charges, buzzed supportively.

They had formed a bond on Zedicon Twelve that could never be broken, a bond forged in the heat of battle underneath a giant eyebrow.

"We are the only ones who know the Eyebrow's secret. Since we've sworn to keep it that way, we're the universe's only hope. We're likely to die out there. Who's with me?"

"I am, Captain!" Fuzzington barked.

"Until the end," Doctor Dirkson said.

"Bzzzz," said General Flirbil.

They all looked at Bera-Bera. His snout-sweat squelched loudly.

"I...I'm in," he said.

"Thank you, everyone."

"Wait!"

Florblap's heart sank into his stomach flap. He'd never heard Steve hesitate before. Steve was the most valuable member of the crew and Florblap couldn't afford to lose him.

"I am the Eyebrow," Steve said.

Florblap burst out laughing and squeezed Steve with a jubilant suction cup.

"Captain?"

"Good Old Steve! Thanks for reminding me. We have to be careful to stay on the right path. There's a little of the Eyebrow in all of us."

"Hear, hear," Doctor Dirkson said.

"Come on, crew. We have work to do."

Steve lingered for a moment. He looked up at his reflection in a space-window. Little hairs had sprouted up in the expanse of skin between two eyebrows; soon there would only be one.

"I tried to warn them," he said. The reflection responded with deep, terror-inducing belly-laughter.

SHIPHOME

Since the liquefaction of Earth, fun has dwindled. If you make me your next ShipHome President, I will personally oversee the return of organized sports.

"Sports? Your platform is sports?" Jenkins knew about sports, but he'd never been interested in doing any. His diet was carefully controlled by his personal robot, just like everyone else's.

"Keep reading," Samuel said.

We will begin with basketball. Basketball was invented during the Boom Age, when humans were out of their minds because they hadn't invented television yet. Organized sports provided the only barrier between humans and the dreaded Obesity monster, a creature so twisted it inflated people like balloons.

"Who wrote this?" Jenkins asked. He'd studied some ancient history in ShipSchool and knew most of that was wrong.

"I did. This speech is going to get me the votes, Jenkins. I'll be ShipHome's next president for sure."

Our basketball games will be played on pavement installed in one of the upper levels. This will come at great expense to the tax payers, namely all of you, but nobody ever got happy by hoarding their money, right?

There are several benefits to playing on pavement, rather than using a non-gravity room. For instance, pavement is cheaper than building a non-gravity arena, and we can pretend there are real streets. You know, like the ones on Earth...or at least how I imagine they must have been.

"Sam...Do you have Cabin Fever?" Jenkins asked. He tried to be cool about it, because Samuel was his friend, but Cabin Fever was the one true terror left to those of ShipHome. They'd abolished crime, disease, and income tax - but the metal hull could never replace a planet.

"I'm not sick. I'm just hopeful."

Jenkins was of the opinion that hope never helped anybody.

"So, what do you think? Should I open it now, or wait until after I've won? What will get me the most votes?" Samuel asked.

Jenkins pushed open the door and surveyed the monstrosity. A large section of the perfectly pleasant ShipTile had been replaced with a strange substance that Samuel identified as "concrete."

"Real outdoor basketball. Can you imagine?"

"No," Jenkins said, because he couldn't. "How did you get Frankson to approve the building permit?" Samuel and Frankson had a long-running hatred of one another, and Jenkins couldn't see him helping Samuel become president.

"Er…Technically he didn't."

"Metal balls! You made a major renovation before consulting Frankson? What the ShipHell were you thinking?" Jenkins wasn't *afraid* of Frankson, exactly, but the man was particular about his "shiny ship." The Chief of Repair and Maintenance took his job seriously.

"Frankson's a stubborn ShipMule. This is going to win me the election," Samuel said.

"If you say so."

"I know so. Now, should I open it right away, or wait? What do you think?"

With a tremendous crash, ShipCeiling fell in large chunks and one almost hit Jenkins before he dodged. He covered his head with his ShipSuit's metal arm. A large metal sphere descended and pounded the basketball court. One section of Samuel's precious concrete was reduced to ShipDust.

"Make your choice, Samuel!" Frankson said, because of course it was Frankson driving the wrecking ball. "You either get rid of this shit and change your platform, or I'll have you disqualified!"

"I can't give in to him, I'll never hear the end of it," Samuel said. He clenched his fists. "I want this, Jenkins. What should I do?"

Jenkins shrugged. "I dunno," he said. "Looks to me like the ball's in your court."

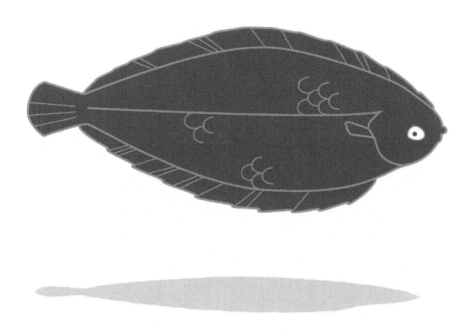

PART 4: AW, COME ON...HUMOUR ME

Contemporary Catastrophes

THE MONTREAL MEAT METAPHOR

Jack and Allen were arguing again. Mary-Anne wasn't surprised; they hadn't gone a day without fighting since the three of them signed the rental agreement. She didn't care if they argued themselves into double murder, but she needed them to shut up so she could study. She slammed the textbook shut and stomped down the stairs.

The tension in the kitchen was palpable, thick and salty, and Mary-Anne could taste the distinct flavour of Montreal smoked meat. She had to admit that as far as arguments went, this one was delicious.

Jack and Allen stood to either side of a silver platter. Jack's left hand was raised and Allen's outstretched right was the angry red of freshly-slapped skin.

Upon the platter was a miracle. Two delectable slices of rye bread, baked only that morning, delicately cradled a massive pile of pink wonder. Smoked havarti had been melted into the crevices of the perfectly smoked meat. A blob of mustard oozed from one side.

"It's just a sandwich," Mary-Anne said.

Allen's left hand crept toward the platter. "This sandwich is a metaphor for our *entire lives*," he said.

"Okay. How?"

Jack slapped the hand so that it had a matching red mark. Allen hissed, and turned to Mary-Anne.

"Imagine Jack and I are trapped in the desert. The ground is barren and there's only one tree but it doesn't have any leaves. Imagine we're the last two men on Earth, and this is the very last sandwich. Who gets the sandwich, Mary-Anne? WHO?"

"Whoever wins the sandwich wins the war," Jack said.

Mary-Anne didn't ask which war. She didn't care enough to listen to

80

another speech. She had a simple solution to their problem.

"Why not split it?"

They gasped in perfect unison. Allen's face actually turned green.

"Right. I forgot. You're both crazy." Mary-Anne sighed. "I don't have time for this, guys. Finals are next week. You should be studying, too. Keep the fight down to a dull roar, yeah?"

"We're almost done here, anyway," Jack said. "This lunch is mine."

"Over my dead body, you - "

Mary-Anne glared.

" - horrible piece of crap," Allen finished in a whisper.

Mary-Anne nodded her approval, and left them to it.

CRASH!

Mary-Anne didn't bother slamming the textbook this time. She hurried down the stairs to stop the inevitable massacre. She had decided that she *did* care if they killed one another, because she didn't want to pay the rent by herself. Oh, and she didn't want to lose her two best friends, but that wasn't as important as the money.

The sandwich was spewed across the floor, smears of mustard forming a frowny face on the tile. The smoked meat was in a neglected pile to the left, and the smoked havarti was on the bottom of Jack's boot.

Jack and Allen were making out on the table.

Mary-Anne went to the fridge for a snack. She'd already been interrupted; she may as well make good use of her time. Upon the top shelf was a miracle; a container filled to the brim with Montreal smoked meat.

"Idiots," Mary-Anne muttered.

CRASH!

Jack and Allen had landed on the floor, but they appeared to be oblivious. The making out continued with the same ferocity as their fighting. The thin line between love and hate had been crossed.

"You do know there's more meat, right?" she said.

"That's not the point," Allen said. "We're imagining we're the last two men on Earth."

"I told you, whoever gets the sandwich wins the war," Jack said.

Mary-Anne made herself a smoked meat sandwich with the leftovers, thereby winning the war, and left the two of them to finish their metaphor.

ALL OF THE OTHERS

Jack had finally left Rudi.. He'd slipped away in the night, leaving only a note behind:

I'm sick and tired of your BS. If you ever stop being an asshole, give me a call. There's a roast in the freezer. Don't starve, idiot.

One of Rudi's biggest problems was ignoring his health. Jack had dragged him to the doctor when absolutely necessary, but in his absence, Rudi didn't bother. He hurt himself a couple of times on the treadmill and doing some heavy lifting at work, but he was too tough to make a fuss about a sore back.

When he blacked out during practice, his coach insisted he seek medical advice, or he wouldn't be allowed to proceed to the official meet. Rudi had been planning on impressing the sponsor, the rich and powerful Mr. Deyre, in hopes of obtaining a permanent contract. He couldn't miss out on the Games.

"Honestly Doctor, my back's a bit sore, but it'll pass. It always does. Muscles get sore when you use them, right?"

"That's entirely true Rudi, but I'm more worried about your broken leg and the stab wounds," the doctor said.

Rudi was tempted to ignore the doctor's diagnosis, but she put in a call to Rudi's coach and he was forced to sit out of practice until the so-called broken leg had healed.

Collecting worker's comp wasn't a problem, since his injuries were supposedly "clearly visible" (the whole world was against him, apparently) and his boss told him to take as much time as he needed.

Unfortunately, Rudi was prone to extreme boredom. It was only a week before he was out of his mind with restlessness. His home nurse, who had been assigned to check his stab-wound bandages once a week, found him at the bar. He wasn't drinking, because he knew that would interfere with his medication, but he was singing karaoke at the top of his voice. The nurse rescued a room full of weeping victims.

"I need to stay in top form for the Games!" Rudi insisted. He was a little loopy from the medication, and karaoke felt like exercise to him.

"You're going home, sir."

"No! You can't stop me!" Rudi grabbed the nurse and shook. "Who sent you to stop me? Who wants me to lose?"

The nurse got Rudi home, but after that night Rudi was under constant supervision. He became a regular stealth ninja in his efforts to slip past the nurses on duty, and was often found doing strenuous activities like boogie dancing or skiing.

The month of April arrived, with showers in full force as one might expect. The rain was a key element in the Games, as Mr. Deyre's favourite sport was umbrella jousting. Rudi was exceptional at it, and had been practicing in secret the entire time he was supposed to be resting. Before he was allowed back on the team, he was forced into a final check-up.

"Well, Rudi, I have good news and bad news," the doctor said. "The good news is that I'm going on vacation in a few days."

"And the bad?"

"The bad news is that you've screwed up your leg so much that it's never going to heal properly."

Rudi tried to prove that he was still as fit as ever, but it turned out that his success during training had been somewhat imagined. He had been jousting from a recumbent position the entire time. (Damn meds.) The doctor was right and he could barely walk, never mind joust.

"Please, give me something. Anything!" Rudi pleaded.

But the Games were for the fit (and less stupid), and alas, Rudi's time was done; no matter how much he begged, they never let poor Rudolph join in any Rain Deyre Games.

POOR THINGS

Zob-Thing took Grub-Thing's suitcases and stacked it with his own. They had only brought the essentials, like eating-things and drinking-things. The rest had been left behind, along with their pride.

Grub-Thing looked around and a disappointed quiver vibrated through his mouth-flaps. Zob-Thing's mouth-flaps wheezed empathetically.

He clenched his hairy fist-bumps angrily. This was such a step down from their last accommodation and he was insulted that they had come to this.

"I am sorry, Friend-Thing," Zob-Thing said.

It was not fair to Grub-Thing that he should be here. He was the heir to the Thing-Throne and had been cast out in disgrace like a Non-Thing. It was Zob-Thing's fault the venture had not been fruitful, and Zob-Thing's fault that money had been lost.

Zob-Thing was willing to take the blame and he was prepared to make up for his actions. He only wished he had not brought dear Grub-Thing down with him.

"Do not despair, Friend-Thing," Grub-Thing said. He put his elbow-sac on Zob-Thing's shoulder-bump. "You are my most important Thing. I would have gone anywhere with you."

"Thank you, Grub-Thing. It does not look like much yet, but it shall be home. We shall plant and harvest Thing-Peppers. We shall invite Other-Things to dine. We shall be rich and popular."

"I miss being popular," Grub-Thing admitted, 'But I know that I will be so again. It is not your fault that the venture failed, my Dear-Thing. Never blame yourself for the incompetence of the others."

"The Other-Things should not have been so angry. We will show them," Zob-Thing said.

Grub-Thing's mouthflaps smiled. Zob-Thing was glad that he could still bring cheer to his Friend-Thing's heart. Grub-Thing always brought so much love to his, and he was not often able to return the favour.

"Do you think they are all up above, feasting on Mini-Things and laughing at us?" Zob-Thing asked.

"Even if they are, and even though this is a step down, it is a place where we can be happy together. The Other-Things will be jealous one day. You'll see," Grub-Thing said.

Zob-Thing was touched. He had ruined Grub-Thing's princely career, and yet he could still smile. Grub-Thing was a treasure.

They were going to need his optimism. Moving down mean that they now lived on Miriam the Human-Thing's backside.

THE PARTING OF WAYS

"Morning, Steve! You're looking good today." Phil likes to start every day with a compliment. There's nothing like good cheer to get the juices flowing.

"Morning, Phil. Is that a new hairdo?" Steve asks.

"Sure is!" Phil is touched that Steve noticed. The wind changed directions yesterday and blew his hairs in a whole new direction. He thinks it suits him and he hopes the wind stays, at least until he gets photographed by a few more tourists.

For a while they chat about the weather. Phil wants to say something comforting about Steve's sister falling, but it only happened yesterday. That wound might be too fresh. Steve is his best friend; when he's ready to talk about her, he will.

Phil has a problem of his own. It's a question for which he's not sure he wants the answer. This is Steve, though (good old Steve), and he'll be polite, but honest. Honesty is what Phil needs right now. He doesn't want to fret - he tries to be as sunny as the sky overhead - but he needs to know.

"I feel fuller than yesterday," Phil says quietly. "Do I look bloated to you?"

Steve pauses. Silence speaks volumes.

"I do, don't I? I look bloated. Damn it, Steve! Damn it!" Phil doesn't enjoy panicking. It makes him leak. Wetting oneself is about as embarrassing as it gets up here.

"No, Phil! Think positive! We promised we'd always be together," Steve says. He might be weeping a little. It's hard to tell through his solid exterior. Phil bets Steve has never leaked a day in his life.

"There's no point in thinking positive now, Steve. I'm going to end up just like..." Phil doesn't want to say *your sister* because that's a low blow. He

86

loves Steve. He doesn't want to part on these terms.

"I'll miss you too much," Steve whispers.

"Steve…Oh Steve, I'm going to miss you, too. I'm so sorry," Phil says. He wishes he had a choice. He doesn't want to abandon Steve so soon after his sister has gone. It's not up to him, though. He's almost ripe.

"You can't! You can't!" Steve cries.

But there is no stopping gravity.

"I love you, Steve!" Phil says.

"I love you too, Phil. Goodbye!"

Phil feels the snap at his head, and soon he's falling. The ground rushes up to greet him and he weeps at the loss of his tree-life. He will miss Steve dearly, but his next adventure is beginning.

Sally picks up the fallen coconut. It's ripe and it looks delicious.

WALLOWING

He knew he heard a scream, but when he turned around he was surprised to see no one was there. An alpaca shuffled up the alley, head cocked to one side curiously. Jeff had heard of screaming goats, but he wasn't sure about alpacas. Was this the owner of the scream?

"Where'd you come from?" Jeff asked.

The alpaca's body heaved. His eyes lit with red fire. He screamed the scream of a thousand death-wailing banshees. Jeff tried to back away and hit the wall.

Something round rolled up the alpaca's long throat. Jeff watched it with horrified fascination. Had it eaten a human head? Was this some terrible nightmare, from which he would wake, only to find he'd wet the bed?

The alpaca ejected a whole orange from its mouth. The fruit splattered to death on the ground at Jeff's feet.

"That's much better," the alpaca said. He spat a great glob of yellow fluid beside the orange's carcass.

"I stopped doing drugs twenty years ago. What's going on?" Jeff demanded.

"I'm here to offer you a choice, Jeff. Will you emerge from the muddy lake of your life and become the Chosen One - or will you wallow in the murky depths and continue on as you are?"

"What's wrong with the way I am?"

"You're a loser, Jeff."

Jeff's job at the factory was far from glamorous, his wife had left him for the pool boy, and his son hardly ever wrote - but he was not a loser. He worked hard for his money, he was dating a charming woman, and his daughter adored him. Jeff chose to focus on the positives of life rather than dwell on the negatives.

"We need you, Jeff. We need a man who is pathetic, has nothing to lose, and is dying to prove himself. You are that man. You will be a hero."

Jeff didn't like the alpaca's tone. Besides, he felt like a hero every time he put the finishing bolts into some safety equipment. He didn't need an orange murderer's approval for a sense of self-worth.

"I'll pass, but thanks for asking," he said.

The alpaca hacked up a banana, an apple, and a grapefruit. His furry expression was one of surprise.

"No one ever refuses! You can't!" the alpaca said.

"You said I had a choice. I'm going to wallow, thanks."

Cherry, cherry, cherry, went the alpaca's throat. Jeff heard the loud ding ding whirr of a slots machine; it looked like he'd won the jackpot. The alpaca screamed one more time and exploded into a plethora of fruit salad.

All that remained of the creature was a small ball of wool, miraculously spun and reading for knitting. Jeff didn't know much about magic or Chosen Ones, but he did know how to knit.

It was the softest gosh darn sweater he'd ever worn.

TRUTH

The "truth serum" was scotch and the "lie detector" was made from junkyard scraps. Jordan was wrapped in several layers of black garbage bags, held together with happy face packing tape. He was wearing gloves, presumably to conceal his fingerprints, but they were the fingerless kind and completely pointless.

Max seriously doubted Jordan's sanity. He was playing along because of Jordan's gun.

"Where is the microfilm, Max?"

"Really? Microfilm? Like in all the spy movies?"

The gun clicked. Max didn't know anything about firearms but clicks were worrisome.

"I don't have it!"

"BEEEEP!" Jordan screeched, acting as the "lie" noise. He squeezed the broken wire that was hooked up to Max's arm and made oil squirt on Max's face.

"Anderson took it!" Max didn't know anyone named Anderson but he was willing to try anything.

"I knew it! That damned traitor!"

"So...can I go now?"

"No, Max, you can't go. You lost the microfilm."

"I don't even know what microfilm is!"

Jordan shoved Max in a closet and locked him in. Max said hello to the darkness.

The light blinded him for a moment, but when he realized the door was open, Max wept for joy. He didn't know how many days he'd been inside, but the darkness was certainly not his friend.

Talking was painful, due to Max's parched throat, but he croaked out the burning question.

"How long?"

"How long what?" Jordan asked. He wasn't wearing any plastic now, but he still held the damn gun, damn him.

"How long was I in there?"

"I don't know, a couple of hours? I brought Anderson," Jordan said. He pointed to the tall man gagged and bound on the floor. Max didn't know if he was dead or unconscious. Surprisingly, he recognized the guy; he'd been a waiter at the restaurant.

"The microfilm was stashed at his apartment," Jordan said.

"It was...what?"

"He had it under a pile of books about the weather. As if that would throw me off the scent!" Jordan kicked Anderson's prone form. "Take that, you prophetic piece of shit."

"What is even going on right now?" Max asked.

"Don't think this absolves you of any guilt. You lost the microfilm in the first place. What do you think would have happened if Magnus had found it?"

"I honestly have no idea, but I'm assuming something bad?"

"Stop playing the fool, Max!" Jordan said. He picked up a foam finger, the kind people buy at sports events, and slapped Max in the face with it. It tickled, but Max pretended to be hurt. (Jordan still had the gun, after all.)

"Talk, Max! Tell me who hired you!"

"Uh...Simpson?"

"Simpson! That son of a - "

Gunshots exploded into the silence of the warehouse. Red blossomed on Jordan's shoulder and he went down. Footsteps hurried Max's way, and a stranger cut his hands free of the rope.

"Thanks," Max said. "But, uh, who are you?"

"I'm Simpson," said the woman.

"Okay."

"Magnus is dead. Jones must have killed him, and now he's on the run."

"I don't..."

"Where's the microfilm, Max?"

"Jordan's got it...Look, can I go now?" Max didn't ask how Simpson knew his name. He didn't care anymore.

"I'll take you home," Simpson said. She checked Jordan's pockets and grabbed something small, presumably the microfilm. She took Max's arm and hurried him outside to her car.

Her tires had been slashed. A man with yet another gun was pointing it at their heads.

"Hello, Simpson."

"Cranberg! You're supposed to be dead!"

"Yet here I am, in the flesh," Cranberg said. "Where's the microfilm, Max?"

"Goddamnit," Max said. "If I live through this, I'm never going on a blind date again."

HAVE ANOTHER

It wasn't supposed to be like this.

Every time the second hand ticks you die a little more inside. You haven't been able to take your eyes off the clock for a solid hour. The professor is still droning on about flora or fauna or something; you don't care. You can't even remember what class you're in right now. You vaguely remember signing up for university in the distant past. Your parents said they were proud of you.

Would they still be proud if they could see you now?

You shift uncomfortably in your seat.

It wasn't supposed to be like this.

"Go on, have another," John said.

You like John. John is handsome and talented and sometimes he helps with your homework. You don't actually need help with your homework but it's nice to lean over the books with him. You've liked him since you met him at the beginning of the year. He's nice to you. He sits down to talk with you. Your friends like him. He likes your friends. He's also handsome.

"Go on, have another," he said. He held it out for you. He smiled and you saw that dimple you like so much.

You took another because you didn't want to tell him the truth.

Did the professor just say something about a purple rhinoceros? Why on Earth would any of your lectures involve a purple rhinoceros…Oh. You must be hallucinating. Your body is so uncomfortable it's trying to amuse itself with whimsical images.

Your body might be amused, but your emotions ache.

If only you could speed up time, or teleport yourself out of the classroom. You know if you get up and leave, the professor will call you out in front of everyone. You've seen it before. You would have to explain, and the explaining might do you in.

Ugh. Why did you say yes? Is John really that hot?

Well, yeah. But...

Tick, tick, tick, says that second hand. The purple rhinoceros winks at you. You consider giving it the finger, but you don't want anyone to notice.

No, it wasn't supposed to be like this.

If John would only get his act together and admit that he's wildly in love with you, you'd be able to start sharing important information about yourself.

For instance - your lactose intolerance.

Your stomach rumbles. If you don't get out of here soon, you're going to have more to regret than that last slice of pizza.

YOU SHOULD NOT BE DANCING

The entire family had undoubtedly been hit with visible disco fever, but they had been hiding it in other ways.

Jennifer's toe was often a-tapping at work, and her body wriggled of its own accord, but she kept the music to a low hum. Her boss never noticed, and some of her coworkers thought she was a bit eccentric, but they didn't know.

Mary worked from home while she took care of the baby, so she only had to hide it when she went out. She could spin and point up/point down to her heart's content, so long as she didn't toss her infant child into the air. (It only happened once, completely by accident, and afterwards Mary swore not to dance while feeding or changing.)

For a time, Jennifer and Mary thought they'd hidden their affliction for the world. Alas, it was not to be.

It exploded into chaos when little Johnny, only eight years old, succumbed to the fever at school. Several arm waves and a hip thrust later, Jennifer and Mary were in the principal's office while she looked down her nose and waited for an explanation.

She couldn't meet the principal's eye. She stared down at the aloe vera plant, wilting sadly on the desk. Even the plant was disappointed in her as a mother. She glanced quickly at Mary, whose arms were folded defensively.

"We caught it from my dad," Jennifer said, before Mary's temper could get the better of her. "He was dancing, and I asked why, and...he said it was how he's staying alive."

"This is unacceptable," the principal said. "Such crude behaviour is entirely inappropriate for someone Johnny's age."

"The fever will pass eventually," Jennifer said. "It has to, right? Disco's dead."

Mary took off her sunglasses and put them on the desk. She let her stylish fur coat slide off her shoulders onto the chair. Underneath, her glittery one-piece bell-bottom suit gleamed in the office lights.

"Disco will never die. Our days shall be filled with dancing, our nights filled with boogie, for the rest of our lives," Mary said. She pointed one finger regally to the sky.

"You can't do that in here -" the principal began, but it was too late.

At least, that's how the story goes.

Whatever happened that day, the disco fever spread rapidly and was so severe that the town had to be quarantined. Experts watched with binoculars from a safe distance for weeks, but the boogying and jiving never let up. They sectioned the town off and condemned it - but days later it was up in flames like a fiery inferno of disco. It could have been an accident - but that's a little too convenient.

It makes you wonder, what really happened in the 70s? Did disco die because it was terrible…or did someone stop it?

Maybe we'll never know.

ROUGE AND NOIR

INTERROGATION ROOM #1

"When did you meet Richardson?"

She waltzed into the room, all legs, in a button-up red shirt. Jack was behind her, and the look in his eyes was both pleading and angry. I know what he was thinking, and I agreed. The woman looked dangerous.

She took a seat in the chair and crossed her long legs (which would have been more entertaining had she been wearing a red dress). I leaned forward and took in the scent of her expensive perfume.

"I hear you're good at finding things," she said.

"It's my specialty," I said. I slipped her one of my cards:

MIRANDA SOUNDERY
Private Detective
If you lost it, I'll find it, guaranteed!*
(I'm also a big hit with the ladies)
555-2142
*Not actually guaranteed

"What have you lost, Miss...?"

"Richardson. Call me Scarlet." She lit up a cigarette and smoke wreathed her blonde hair. "I'll pay you handsomely to recover my lost heirloom."

"What is it, and how did you lose it?"

"It's called the Black Sapphire. It was stolen."

Black sapphire isn't an expensive stone, but I wasn't interested why she wanted it back. If it was a family heirloom, it might have sentimental value. All I care about is finding the thing and getting paid for finding the thing. I wouldn't have become a private detective if I wasn't interested in money.

"Burglary is usually a job for the police," I said.

"Yes, but I don't trust the police to be as discreet," Scarlet said. "I don't want this staining my family name, you see."

I didn't know which Richardson family she belonged to, but I could think of several that had plenty of money.

"When was it taken?" I asked.

She puffed a ring of smoke in my face. "Three nights ago. I thought I could locate it myself, but I had no such luck. You are my only hope now, Miranda. What do you think?"

"I think you can't smoke in here, this is a public building," I said.

"About the case, detective."

"Oh, that. Yeah, I'll do it," I said. Jack was glaring at me with his murder-eyes, but I ignored him. He was always lecturing me about taking cases before getting the details. It got me into trouble more than once. I like trouble, but Jack never did. He was a good assistant though, the best I'd ever had.

I have good reason to forego the details when the client is a beautiful woman, though.

"Are you free tonight?" Scarlet asked. "We can discuss the details over a drink."

I told her I'd be delighted.

INTERROGATION ROOM #2

"Tells me about Scarlet Richardson."

Scarlet Richardson...how can I describe her? Six feet tall, blonde, athletic, busty; she had it all. When I saw her sitting at the bar in a little red dress, I knew Miranda was doomed. She's a sucker for a woman in red, especially one as attractive as Scarlet.

Taking the case was her first mistake.

Her second? Going on that date with Scarlet. She should have known trouble follows her wherever she goes.

I tailed her to Garnet bar and watched them drink and flirt for hours. Miranda was happy as a kid in a candy store by the time they were through, and she invited Scarlet back to her place.

Look, I'm no voyeur, but I didn't trust Scarlet, okay? Miranda lived above the shop so I waited in her office while they had their alone time. When I heard footsteps on the stairs, I went out to look and there she was - Scarlet Richardson, hands full of Miranda's secret files. She also had a pair of Miranda's underwear, but that's none of my business.

I stopped her; what else was I supposed to do? I didn't hit her. I called her name. She stopped dead in her tracks, looked at me, and smiled.

That's when she shot me.

INTERROGATION ROOM #1

"What happened after your date?"

I heard a gunshot so I ran downstairs. Jack was passed out on the floor and his leg was bleeding. It wasn't a major wound, he's had worse, but he'd hit his head on the way down.

I bandaged him up and woke him with some cold water to the face.

"What the hell just happened?" he said.

"I was going to ask you the same thing," I said.

"Scarlet Richardson just *shot* me, Miranda! What were you thinking, bringing her here? She stole some of our documents!"

"No, she didn't. I gave them to her," I said. She'd expressed interest in private detecting. I wasn't about to be rude to my house guest. Sure, she didn't want to stay the night, but they never do. My place is next to a fish factory.

"You can't give out our files like that! We have a client confidentiality clause," Jack said.

"Yeah, yeah. Who's going to check?" I said.

Jack just made some disgusted noise, so I took him to the hospital.

INTERROGATION ROOM #2

"Tell me how you found the warehouse."

Miranda got me discharged from the hospital a couple hours later. I'd just been shot, but she has connections.

Have I mentioned I hate her?

The next day we asked around about the Black Sapphire. We went to a few of the people Scarlet listed as potential enemies. Most of them were rich, busy, and pissed we were taking up their time, but one of them gave us a clue. It was an abandoned warehouse - of course it was an abandoned warehouse! - where one of their clients made cheap, ugly jewelry. Miranda was all fired up to go down there.

"What if it's a trap?" I asked.

"You watch too many movies," she said.

So we went to the warehouse anyway. Guess what? It was a trap.

There were guns and grenades and we were unarmed. I have no idea who all those people were but for some reason they wanted us dead.

Miranda pulled one of her fancy moves and got her hands on a grenade. We hid behind a stack of aluminum barrels. I tried to block out the sounds of shooting and our eventual death.

"It seems Scarlet was hiding something," Miranda said.

"No, really? What was your first clue?" I said.

"Where's the Black Sapphire?" one of the shooters demanded.

"We're here to ask you the same thing!" Miranda said.

"We know she took it, and she went to you! Hand it over!"

"Miranda," I said. "Did Scarlet leave something in your apartment?"

Miranda shrugged. "How should I know? I can never find anything under all the piles of dirty laundry."

"You can't hide it from us! We're taking the Black Sapphire poison, and we're going to wipe out all of the Richardsons!" another shooter yelled.

"Oh. That makes so much more sense than a shitty gem," Miranda said. She chucked the grenade. That's how those four bodies showed up in the warehouse.

INTERROGATION ROOM #1

"Now the explosion."

Jack quit on me after the grenade incident. I was disappointed in his lack of loyalty and tried to convince him to stay. I didn't want to let go of the best assistant I ever had.

He told me where to put my job and he took off. I thought I'd never see him again. I didn't hire a new assistant though, on the slim chance he'd come back to me.

I tried to give Scarlet a call, but she wouldn't pick up. She wouldn't pick up for three days. I left her a couple of messages explaining why we didn't have her gem back yet. I started getting suspicious.

I did a little digging on the Richardsons. Turns out they and another family, the Dennissons, have been feuding for decades. The feud seemed to center around this cheap black stone.

I didn't get it.

When the phone rang that afternoon, I thought it would be Scarlet. It wasn't. It was Jack.

"I'm glad you called," I said. "I think Scarlet's trouble, Jack," I said.

"No shit," he said, and that's when I heard the explosion.

100

"It was your house that exploded. Why?"

Believe me, I'd love to know why. It happened not long after I quit Miranda's agency. I couldn't get Scarlet Richardson and the bad feeling out of my head, even though I'd sworn it wasn't my business anymore. I did some digging, and found out she was part of a feud that had been going on for generations. She was young, but she was the head of the Richardsons, and my connections informed me that she was singlehandedly responsible for at least fifty deaths.

I wrote up everything I could find and locked it in my desk. When it was done, I decided to call Miranda. I hate her, but I didn't want her to die.

My drawer wasn't locked anymore.

Scarlet's files were missing, as well as most of my petty cash. The thief had left me a calling card, though; a black gem with a ribbon tied around it.

I called Miranda from outside my house.

"I think Scarlet's trouble, Jack," she said.

"No shit," I said.

My house exploded into smithereens. I'm lucky I wasn't injured. I still don't know where Scarlet Richardson or her family is, and you know what? I don't want to know anymore.

"Are you sure?"

Yeah, officer. I'm positive.

"Jack! Don't tell them anything! It's a trap!"

What the...Was that Miranda? Did you bring her in, too? Look, I didn't want to mention it, but this lemonade tastes funny...What are you doing? Gross, don't take off your face - Oh my God.

Scarlet?

"The Black Sapphire isn't a gem, Jack. It's the family's secret recipe for untraceable poison."

Is that why the lemonade tastes funny?

"No."

Thank God you didn't poison me!

"Of course I poisoned you! The poison is tasteless. The lemonade tastes funny because it's expired."

Well, ain't that just a kick in the pants!

AUBERGINE
(Eggplant)

Rita wouldn't put haunted woods on her top ten list of places to hang out, but it wasn't as bad as the haunted port-a-potty from a few minutes earlier. The faint light of the moon outlined old, gnarled trees, and her breath made steam on the air. The ambience might have been charming, if the damn elephants would stop cycling.

"They're too heavy for the bikes. It's painful to watch," Rita remarked to the rattle-spider. Its name was Janet and it had a fake Australian accent.

"Crikey!" Janet said.

"Weren't there two of you earlier?" Rita asked.

"Well sure, but you said you were hungry."

"Uh...so?"

"So you ever tried a rattle-spider burger? Delicious, mate!"

Rita realized there was a burger in her hands. She'd met the meat earlier, but there was cheese and bacon so she let that slide.

It was delicious.

"As far as dreams go, I've had worse," she admitted.

Janet shook the rattle at the end of her tail. She dashed up Rita's arm with her tickly spider legs. Sharp teeth punctured Rita's neck.

"Ow! What the...?"

The pain didn't wake her.

"What is this feeling?" Rita asked. "There's this...this creeping fear inside me. It's just a dream, why should I be scared?"

"It isn't a dream, mate."

"That's ridiculous. What else would this be? There are cycling elephants, for goodness' sake."

"It's reality, obviously," Janet said.

The rattle-spider's poison pulsed through Rita's veins. The dark purple liquid stained her from the inside and out. Her body stretched to impossible angles and green leaves sprouted from the top of her head.

She was turning into an eggplant!

"Why is this happening?" the eggplant wailed. "How is this even possible?"

"Dunno mate, but that colour on you is aubergine-ious."

Rita's scream of horror was what finally woke her from the nightmare.

"That's it - no more stoner movies before bed," she decided.

She was so relieved that she didn't see the tip of a rattle retreating beneath her bed.

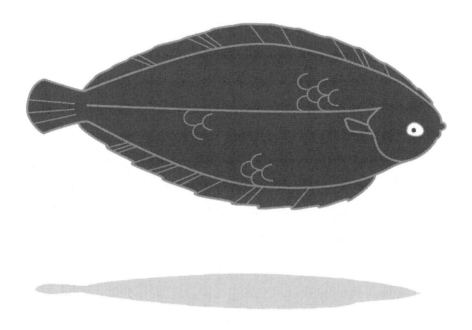

PART 5: PUN FOR THE ROAD

Because how else would I end this book?

SPECIAL BREAKFAST

Old Bill was the first of the Fishchildren line. Most of Old Bill's belongings had been destroyed in the fire of '26 but one or two pictures remained. The one of him by the lighthouse with the massive trout was Harold's favourite.

Old Bill was a master fisher back in the day, but it wasn't fishing that made his fortune. He started the restaurant that made Harold's family rich. They specialized in fresh seafood caught by Old Bill himself. He passed the restaurant on to his son, who passed it to his daughter, and so on down the line until it reached Harold's dad.

Harold was ten years old when his dad got the restaurant. He was raised waiting tables and helping out in the kitchen. His dad taught him everything he'd learned from the family tradition, and Harold became a master chef.

Harold has two dreams that have been with him ever since he learned how to dream: to make his great-great-great-great-great-great grandfather proud of him, and to find true love. His father assures him that he's well on his way to the first wish, and as to the second, Harold has been trying to take care of that as well.

Harold turns on the stove and greases the pan. He gutted and scaled the sole earlier this morning. He kisses the naked creature on both sides, because the family's secret ingredient is *love*.

He sears the fish on both sides for two minutes each. He adds salt and pepper and squeezes a lemon onto the fish. He puts the pan into the oven for another five minutes, and after that he gets out the blowtorch. It isn't part of Old Bill's original recipe, but someone added it along the way and it's crucial to the signature Fishchildren dish.

Old Bill really would be proud of the finished product. It's hot, but not burned. The skin is golden and crispy. The scent of lemon fills the air with sour promise.

Harold knows exactly what time to have the fish ready. He's been dating Mickey for three months and the man wakes up at eight o'clock every day without an alarm. Harold doesn't know how he does it.

They usually stay at Mickey's apartment, because it's in the city. Harold invited Mickey over last night because three months is long enough; it's time for things to get serious. For any Fishchildren child, "serious" means cooking for your loved ones for the first time.

Mickey arrives in the kitchen promptly at eight. Harold passes him the plate and beams with the pride of his ancestors.

"I've made you a special breakfast," Harold says.

"Thanks, Harry, but I don't eat fish," Mickey says. He shrugs casually, like it's no big deal.

Harold's legs stop functioning. He collapses in a chair and presses a hand to his forehead with Woe. He emits a blood-curdling wail.

"What's the matter?" Mickey asks. He kneels at Harold's side like a proper boyfriend, but now Harold knows what's underneath.

"I really thought you were the one," Harold says.

Mickey frowns. "Is there a 'but'?"

"Yes."

"Why? What's the problem?"

"It's not meant to be," Harold says. "You and I, Mickey…We can never be Sole Mates."

107

ABOUT THE AUTHOR

Holly Geely, *noun.* **1.** a Canadian who likes bright colours, bad jokes, and terrible puns **2.** A bookkeeper with four pets who spends too much time playing video games **3.** an avid reader of many genres.

Printed in Great Britain
by Amazon